AVIS DOLPHIN

AVIS DOLPHIN

FRIEDA WISHINSKY
WILLOW DAWSON

Groundwood Books / House of Anansi Press
Toronto / Berkeley

The quotation on page 164 is from "Living at the Edge of the World,"
by John Henley, *The Guardian*, February 21, 2008.

With special thanks to Nan Froman, who helped make *Avis* sail off in style.
— FW

Published in Canada and the USA in 2015 by Groundwood Books

Groundwood Books / House of Anansi Press
110 Spadina Avenue, Suite 801, Toronto, Ontario M5V 2K4
or c/o Publishers Group West
1700 Fourth Street, Berkeley, CA 94710

We acknowledge for their financial support of our publishing program
the Canada Council for the Arts, the Government of Canada through the
Canada Book Fund (CBF) and the Ontario Arts Council.

Canada Council   Conseil des Arts
for the Arts   du Canada

ONTARIO ARTS COUNCIL
CONSEIL DES ARTS DE L'ONTARIO
an Ontario government agency
un organisme du gouvernement de l'Ontario

Library and Archives Canada Cataloguing in Publication
Wishinsky, Frieda, author
Avis Dolphin / written by Frieda Wishinsky ; illustrated by
Willow Dawson.
Issued in print and electronic formats.
ISBN 978-1-55498-489-3 (bound). — ISBN 978-1-55498-490-9 (html).
— ISBN 978-1-55498-813-6 (mobi)
1. Lusitania (Steamship) — Juvenile fiction.
2. Shipwrecks — Juvenile fiction I. Dawson, Willow, illustrator
II. Title.
PS8595.I834A85 2015   jC813'.54   C2014-906748-8
                             C2014-906749-6

The illustrations were done in ink on bristol paper.
Binding and text design by Michael Solomon
Printed and bound in Canada

MIX
Paper from
responsible sources
FSC
www.fsc.org   FSC® C103567

To Sheila and Willow,
who took the journey with me.
With many thanks and many hugs. — FW

For Wolf, whose story is only just
beginning to unfold.
(And to Frieda, Sheila, Michael and Nan.) — WD

Day One
Saturday, May 1, 1915

Morning • The New York City Dock

THE DUSTY FUMES and the fishy smells on the New York dock make me gag, but I can't stop staring at everything.

Shiny black cars and horse-drawn carriages drive up to Pier 54 and deposit their passengers. Porters pile up trunks and suitcases like towers. Some children cling to their parents. Others race up and down the dock, weaving between cars, horses and people. Their parents shout, "Don't wander away. The *Lusitania* is sailing soon." Passengers speak English, French and a bunch of languages I can't name.

The *Lusitania* is called the Big *Lusy*. The name makes the ship sound friendly, even though she's huge and elegant and will soon be full of strangers. Rich strangers, poor strangers and strangers in the middle, like us.

A man and a woman beside me hold each other and kiss. Friends hug goodbye. A father gathers his children close, ready to board the ship.

I wish my father were alive and with me on the dock. I wish I wasn't sailing far from home with Hilda and Sarah. They're nurses who worked at Mother's home for the sick and aged. Mother asked them to look after me on the *Lusitania*, but they don't want to be with me. They want …

Oh no! No!

A horse's hoof scrapes my leg.

No room to move! No place to run. I'm going to be trampled!

"Watch out!"

A man pulls me away. I stumble against his shoulder. I'm trembling, but I manage to straighten up.

"I … I'm sorry," I tell the man. "Thank you."

The man smiles. His eyes are soft and kind. "You had a close call. Be careful," he says in a thick Scottish accent. Before I can say anything, he tips his tweed hat and hurries toward the gangplank of the *Lusitania*.

I turn and there's Hilda.

"What's the matter with you, Avis?" she snaps. "You almost got yourself killed."

"I didn't see the horse. I was … thinking."

"Thinking? Again? Oh, Avis. You do far too much thinking." Hilda gives me her look. The one that makes me feel like she's wagging her finger in my face.

She pats her dark brown hair to make sure that the pins holding her bun are still there. They are, of course. Hilda's hair always stays in place, even on a rainy, misty day like today. Even with people and horses jostling us on the dock. Not like my thick, unruly brown hair. My hair has a mind of its own.

"You don't appreciate your good fortune, Avis!" says Hilda. "How many twelve-year-olds have the chance to travel across the ocean on a magnificent ship like the *Lusitania*? Don't you agree, Sarah?"

Sarah nods. Her blonde curls bob up and down like a yo-yo, but I can tell she hasn't heard a word Hilda said. Sarah's big green eyes are glued to two young men in dark blue suits and crisp white shirts sauntering toward the *Lusitania*.

I know Hilda is right. Sometimes I think too much. I try not to, but it's hard not to think about Father, our home in St. Thomas, or my best friend, Lizzie. It's hard not to wonder what it will be like to be far away at school in England. Far from everything and everyone I know and care about.

If only Lizzie were here. Lizzie and I talk about everything. How bossy my mother is, how her father drinks too much and how her mother cries when he does. How we hate, hate, hate it when Mary Roberts at school parades around in her latest frock and sniffs at us like we're wearing rags. How much we love adventure stories, especially ones about far-off magical lands, even though most of them are about boys. (Why can't someone write one about a girl? Girls love magic and adventure, too.)

I hope I make a friend on the *Lusy*! I don't want to be alone in the middle of the Atlantic with nothing but ocean around me for seven days.

All Hilda and Sarah want to do is meet famous people or flirt with young men. That's all they talked about on the train from Canada. How they'd meet them, what they'd say, what they'd wear.

"Hey, girl. Move out of the way!" A burly photographer with a curly black mustache shoves me forward.

"Don't push," I say, but he doesn't listen. He and his friend barrel ahead, snapping picture after picture of rich and famous celebrities about to board the ship.

"There's that millionaire, Mr. Vanderbilt!" the photographer shouts to his friend. "Can you see his face, George? Does he look worried? Can you get his picture?"

"I don't know," says George. "He's moving quickly but he looks calm. Like he doesn't have a care in the world. I wonder if he's heard the rumors."

"He must have heard. They were plastered all over the newspaper this morning. I saw them right under the announcement that the *Lusitania* is sailing to Liverpool. The words were big, bold and clear. The Germans mean business."

George rolls his eyes. "Maybe if you're rich, you think nothing can harm you."

"Nah. Not after the *Titanic*. Money didn't save

Benjamin Guggenheim, John Astor or Mr. and Mrs. Strauss. The rich die just like the rest of us."

What are they talking about? What rumors? What danger? Why would Mr. Vanderbilt or anyone die on the *Lusitania*?

"Hilda," I say, "did you read the newspapers today? Is the *Lusitania* in danger?"

Hilda is standing on her tiptoes to see Mr. Vanderbilt. "Oh that. Nothing to worry about, Avis." She waves her hand in the air like she's swatting a fly. "I heard that Mr. Sumner, the spokesman for the Cunard company, reassured Mr. Vanderbilt that the *Lusitania* is too fast to be in danger of being torpedoed by German U-boats. It's all rumors and fear-mongering. The press love that. It sells newspapers."

Hilda points in the direction of the two photographers. The burly one glares at her.

My heart pounds like it did when Mother told me I was going to school in England. "But England is far away," I told her, "and it's at war."

"The war is on battlefields in Europe, far from where you'll be living, Avis. And it won't last. A few months more at most and it will be over. You'll be perfectly safe with your grandparents and at school. This is a wonderful opportunity for you to get a good education. It's what your father would have wanted."

What could I say? I didn't want to leave home, but Mother insisted. And now with all this talk about

German U-boats and warnings in the newspaper, I want to jump back on that train.

I know about U-boats. They're submarines hiding under the sea, waiting for ships, like foxes hiding in bushes, waiting to pounce on rabbits or deer. When U-boats spy a warship, they launch a torpedo! And if the ship is hit, that's it. The ship sinks. But until today I thought the U-boats were only after warships.

I tap Hilda on the shoulder. "Maybe the warning is real. Maybe …"

"There you go again, Avis," says Hilda. "Stop worrying! Do you think a millionaire like Mr. Vanderbilt would risk his life sailing on the *Lusitania* if there was anything to be concerned about?"

"Or Lady Mackworth," Sarah chimes in. "She's a suffragette fighting for women's rights. She knows all about politics and what's going on in the world. She wouldn't sail on the *Lusitania* if there was any danger. And neither would Josephine Eaton Burnside, the daughter of Timothy Eaton who owns that department store, or that New York fashion designer, Carrie Kennedy, or …"

"See, Avis," says Hilda, interrupting Sarah. "No one else is letting a few rumors scare them off. All your worrying will just give you a headache. It's already giving me a headache!"

"Enjoy yourself, Avis. I certainly will," says Sarah. "Imagine! We might even meet some famous people on the ship!"

"I hope you ladies *do* enjoy your trip. It may be your last," says the burly photographer.

Hilda glares at him. "What a cruel thing to say," she snaps. "Do you realize you're scaring an impressionable young girl?" Hilda puts her arm around me and squeezes my shoulder so hard that I wince.

"Look. I'm only telling you what I've heard. It's not too late to turn back. You don't have to sail on the *Lusitania*. Some people have canceled their trip."

I untangle myself from Hilda's arm. What if the photographer is right? What if it isn't all fear-mongering, but there's something real to fear? After all, everyone said the *Titanic* was unsinkable, and it sank. How could the Cunard people be sure that nothing is going to happen to the *Lusitania*?

"Hilda," I begin again.

Hilda cuts me off and shakes her finger in the photographer's face. "We have no intention of changing our plans. We are not afraid of rumors."

"Rumors can be true," says the photographer, pointing his camera. With a click he takes a picture of the three of us. "Well, if anything happens at least we have your picture." The photographer and his friend push through the crowd as a black car drives up to the dock and deposits another wealthy couple on their way to the *Lusitania*.

I look up. Smoke curls from three of the four giant smokestacks on the ship. Huge escalators haul up suitcases, trunks and boxes. The gangplanks have been lowered, and people scurry aboard.

"Ready?" says Hilda. Her face is flushed with excitement.

I have no choice. I'm sailing on the *Lusitania*. I close my eyes and try to lock out my frightening thoughts.

"I'm ready," I say.

"Me, too," says Sarah. She smiles so widely I can see all her teeth. She looks like she just won first prize at the fair. "I hope we meet some young men at dinner tonight. Some must be traveling second class like us."

"You and your young men," says Hilda, raising her eyebrows.

"Look! The sun is coming out! Just in time for sailing," says Sarah. "This is going to be a marvelous trip."

The sun pokes through the clouds and glistens on the dock, the ship and the ocean. I peer around. People are smiling.

"What a perfect day to sail," says a woman in a flowing scarlet cloak beside me.

The sun has changed everyone's mood — even mine. Maybe Hilda and Sarah are right. Maybe this will be an amazing adventure. I've never had a *real* adventure — except in books.

I glance up to the deck of the *Lusy*. People on board wave to their friends and family below. Bright, colorful flags fly from the ship. A band plays as Hilda, Sarah and I weave our way through the crowd toward the gangplank. We're almost there when two bellboys in uniforms with shiny brass buttons scoot toward us.

"Have you seen a black cat?" the bellboy with flaming red hair and a face full of freckles asks me.

"No," I say. "Have you lost your cat?"

"It's the ship's cat, Dowie," says the bellboy. "He never goes missing but we haven't seen him all day."

"Dowie always senses danger," says the other bellboy. His round glasses skid off his nose. "Remember when we had the fire in the galley, Sam? Remember how Dowie wouldn't stop meowing till we had a look? Dowie knows when something bad is going to happen. Maybe that's why he's run off."

"Maybe Dowie is already on the *Lusitania*," I say.

Sam pats his friend on the back. "Right, Lou. That's probably all it is."

"I hope so, miss," says Lou. He sighs and adjusts his glasses again. "Let's hurry, Sam. We're going to be late. Then we'll be in real trouble."

I walk up the gangplank beside Hilda and Sarah. The ocean, so dull and gray just a few hours ago, is sparkling and as blue as the sky. Everyone is saying goodbye.

"Write soon."

"Stay safe."

"Don't eat too much!"

"Don't have too much fun!"

A man in a brown suit ahead of me turns to his companion. "All this fuss about the Germans is nonsense."

"I know," says his friend. "The Germans wouldn't dare torpedo a ship with so many American passengers aboard. If they did it would catapult America into the war. That's the last thing Germany wants."

His friend nods. "You're right. The *Lusitania* is safer than a New York trolley car."

The men laugh. Their laughter makes me feel safer. And when we reach the deck, I feel even better. Everyone around me looks excited and happy. Everyone wants to see what the ship looks like. They can't wait to taste the food, meet new people, stroll the deck and enjoy the ocean breeze. And suddenly, neither can I!

A girl of about seven with curly brown hair turns to me. "Do you think we'll see whales and dolphins on the trip?"

I smile. "I hope so. That would be wonderful, especially since my last name is Dolphin."

"Dolphin!" says the girl. "That means you belong at sea."

"Maybe I do," I say.

At 11:30 a.m. the all-ashore gong sounds. Visitors pour off the deck.

Goodbye, New York.

Goodbye, home!

We are about to sail.

Afternoon • On the Deck

AT 12:20 P.M. the *Lusy* finally pulls out from the dock. I'm so busy watching everything that I jump when the three shrill horn blasts announce that we're moving. People on shore wave their hats and hand-kerchiefs. Confetti rains down on my hair, my bow, my collar and all over my dress. A band plays "It's a Long Way to Tipperary," and then Welsh singers belt out "The Star Spangled Banner."

Sarah clasps her hands. "Isn't this a fantastic par-ty!" she says. "I can see by your smile that you're en-joying it, too, Avis."

It's true. I love the confetti, the singers, and the sun warming my face. I've never sailed on a huge, fancy ship like the *Lusy*, but I love being out on the water.

Sometimes Lizzie and I paddle her canoe on the lake near our house. We love to drift, watch clouds change their shape, listen to birds and talk about the adventures we will have one day. If Lizzie were here with me now, we'd explore every inch of this ship together. She'll want to know everything about the *Lusy* when I write her.

The *Lusy* passes the pier in Hoboken, New Jersey, and the American ship, the *New York*. We glide by three camouflaged British warships. They remind me that Britain is at war with Germany, and the Ger-mans warned us not to sail. But then the seamen from a British ship sling bags of mail aboard the *Lu-sitania*, and I feel better. The British believe the mail will arrive safely. And if the mail arrives in one piece, so will we!

"Here comes the mail!" I say.

"And the *Lusy* will deliver it on time," says Sarah.

"Absolutely," says a tall, mustached man with a strong English accent. "The British Admiralty will escort us safely to Liverpool when we near shore. They'll want to prevent those German U-boats from harming our ships and our post."

We grin and nod to each other, confident that all will be well.

"Come on," says Hilda. "Let's see our cabins." She gives my arm a gentle squeeze as the three of us head down a long corridor.

We peek into salons filled with carved mahogany tables and thick rose-colored carpets. We *ooh* and *ahh* at glass domes and painted murals. We marvel at the chandeliers twinkling like stars. I love the deep, soft sofas and the big, throne-like chairs. I promise myself that I will sink into one of them tomorrow and read my new book about two boys on their way to an enchanted land who are captured by pirates.

"The *Lusy* is a floating palace!" I say.

"See," says Hilda, giving me one of her looks. "I told you to stop worrying."

Why does Hilda have to speak to me like I'm a child? I hate it, but I don't say anything.

We find our second-class cabin. It's small, but everything is neat and pretty. There are four bunk beds, two on either side of gleaming white double sinks with a big mirror. There are cabinets in the walls for storing our clothes.

"Why don't you take that top bunk, Avis?" says Hilda. "Children love the top bunk."

"I am not a child," I want to shout at her, but the truth is that I do like sleeping on top. It's cozy. I like the privacy curtains and the little metal basket to store small items that is attached to the wall beside each berth.

"OK," I agree.

"Good!" says Hilda, lounging on the bottom bunk opposite mine. "Sarah, you don't mind sleeping under Avis, do you?"

"I'd rather sleep over there." Sarah points to the berth Hilda is lying on. "But I'll be a good sport. You don't snore, do you, Avis?"

"No," I say.

"Well, if you do, I'll just kick your bed and that will stop you."

Sarah and Hilda giggle.

I don't think it's funny.

Sarah unpacks her toiletries, and Hilda unpacks her clothes and stores them in the cabinets. I pull out my nightgown and lay it on the bedspread with the Cunard emblem on it.

Then Hilda and Sarah discuss what to wear for dinner.

"The blue?"

"The purple?"

"The black?"

They debate the merits of each dress in endless detail. They talk on and on and on, and I am bored. Bored! Bored! I'm about to tell them that I'm going out to take a walk on deck when they finally make up their minds.

When it's time to get ready for dinner, Hilda puts on a black dress that's so severe and has so many tiny buttons, she looks like she's going to a funeral. I don't tell her that.

Sarah chooses a blue dress. It makes her look fussy with all its ribbons and bows. I don't tell her that, either.

"Aren't you changing, Avis?" asks Hilda. "What about the dark green dress you wore at Easter? It looks good with your brown eyes. That dark blue you have on is so drab."

Why is Hilda telling me how to dress? She's as bossy as Mother.

"I like this blue dress and I'm not changing," I say.

"It was just a suggestion, Avis," she snaps. "I only want to help you look your best. Appearances matter on a ship like the *Lusitania*. Don't you agree, Sarah?"

Sarah bobs her head up and down. "Absolutely," she says, sliding a jangly blue bracelet up her arm. "I try to look my best at all times."

Hilda gives a last touch to her perfect hair. "Let's go."

We make our way to the second-class dining room. Long tables are set with gleaming white cloths and crisp napkins. Stately pillars and tall plants surround the tables, and thick carpets cushion our feet. The chairs are soft, and they swivel!

There's a young man with curly blond hair and a mustache at one end of the table, and Sarah dashes over to the seat beside him. She introduces herself and begins to talk. She's still talking when the first course arrives. It's creamy potato soup. We all begin to eat, except Sarah. She's too busy flirting with the young man, whose name is Stephan. He isn't saying much. Maybe that's because Sarah doesn't let him. She talks on and on.

Poor Stephan. I doubt he will ever want to sit near us again.

Evening • Ha!

I WISH I COULD sleep, but thoughts of Father, home, Lizzie, England, my grandparents, the trip on the *Lusy* spin around in my head like a merry-go-round. Will I like my new school? Will I make friends? Are we safe here? Will Hilda and Sarah ever stop snoring?

I turn over, trying to drown out their snores. I twist a pillow around my head to muffle the noise. But it doesn't help. They snort. They whoosh. They snort again and again. And they were worried I would snore. Ha!

I want to sleep. I'm so, soooo tired after the train ride from Canada, the crowds and noise on the dock, the horse that almost trampled me, the worry, the buzz on the ship and all the food at dinner. I have to sleep. I have to …

Day Two
Sunday, May 2, 1915

Morning • First Day at Sea

OH NO! THE CABIN is spinning! And so is my head! And my stomach aches like someone is churning butter inside it.

Sarah raps my legs. "Get up, lazy bones," she says. "It's our first breakfast on the *Lusitania* and I don't want to miss a minute. If it's anything like supper last night, it will be delicious."

Hilda and Sarah are already dressed.

"I feel sick," I say.

"It's just a touch of seasickness," says Hilda. "The *Lusy* can roll but you'll get used to it. Come on. Try and stand up. I'll help you." Hilda holds out her hand.

I take deep breaths. I try to push down the queasiness rushing up to my throat. I sit up and slowly swing my legs over the berth. I hold Hilda's hand and slide to the floor. She helps me slip into my stockings and dress.

"Hurry," says Sarah, heading to the door.

"We can't move any faster, Sarah. Avis is not feeling well," says Hilda. She gives Sarah one of her looks.

Sarah winces. "I don't mean to be unkind, Avis," she says. "It's just that we don't want to miss a moment of anything. Especially not breakfast."

I groan. If this is what I'm going to feel like for the rest of the trip, I can miss all of it. I splash cold water on my face. I swish cold water around in my mouth, but I still feel queasy.

"Ready?" says Hilda.

I nod. I do feel a little better as we walk to the dining room. The swivel chairs were fun last night, but today the thought of swiveling makes my stomach turn over. I wish I was on solid ground. I wish I felt better.

Stephan, the young man whom Sarah flirted with last night, is already seated. Sarah scurries over to sit beside him. He glances up briefly and mutters, "Hello." Then he looks down at his glass of juice as if he's studying it for an exam.

"How are you, Stephan?" Sarah coos.

"Well, thank you," he replies. Now his eyes are glued to the cutlery as if it were made of gold.

"I am very well, too, Stephan," says Sarah. She tells him how lovely our cabin is, how well she slept, what a gorgeous day it is, how beautiful the *Lusitiania* is and on and on and on.

Stephan says nothing.

"I'll have the corned beef hash, hominy cakes and oodles of that luscious golden syrup," Sarah tells the waiter.

"Lamb chops and fried potatoes for me," says Hilda.

Stephan looks up briefly and orders toast, one fried egg and black coffee.

"And you, young lady?" the waiter asks me.

"A piece of toast, please," I mutter.

"Just toast. That's all?"

I nod.

"I understand," he says.

Even before the toast arrives, my queasy feeling gets worse. I must be turning a gruesome shade of green because Hilda leans over and whispers, "Why don't you go out on the deck for air, Avis? I'll check on you after breakfast."

I can barely nod. I stand up *very* slowly. I don't want to be sick all over the white tablecloth. What would Hilda and Sarah say then! Think of something else, I tell myself as I head to the deck. Anything else. Picking daisies in the garden at home. Swimming in the lake on a summer day. Reading under the tall maple tree.

I make it to the deck and sink into a chair. The ship isn't rocking hard. It's just a steady back and forth, but it's enough to make me queasy. I have to get used to this rocking motion. But how? No one else on deck seems bothered by it.

I breathe slowly — in and out. In and out. I look straight ahead. I don't move my head. If I do, I'll throw up.

"Excuse me, young lady," says a man in a thick Scottish accent. "Didn't we bump into each other near a horse on the dock?"

I recognize the voice and the accent. I lift up my head slowly. It's the man who saved me from being trampled! He's wearing the same tweed cap and tweed coat.

"I'm Ian Holbourn," he says, tipping his cap like he did yesterday. "You look seasick."

I nod.

"Have you ever sailed before?"

"Not on the ocean."

"Ah, you'll get your sea legs soon. My youngest son was seasick for years but he gradually outgrew it. You will, too. Meanwhile, you might do something to distract yourself. Why don't you join me for a walk?"

Mr. Holbourn seems so nice and a walk might help. "OK," I agree. I grasp the sides of the chair and pull myself up. I take deep breaths, and as I do, I see Hilda and Sarah coming toward me. "I'm taking a walk with Mr. Holbourn," I tell them. My voice is shaky.

"Professor Ian Holbourn?" exclaims Hilda. "The Laird of Foula?"

Mr. Holbourn laughs. "You know who I am?"

"I read about you in the ship's bulletin. You're

speaking to the passengers on Wednesday. The bulletin says that you've given over a thousand lectures across the United States. And you're a writer, an explorer and the laird of an island in Scotland, too."

"It's only a wee island," says the professor.

"What's a laird? Is that like a king?" I ask.

"It means I own the island and I'm in charge of its affairs," says Professor Holbourn. "Now you know my name but I don't know yours."

"I'm Avis Dolphin."

"And I'm Hilda Ellis and this is Sarah Smith. We're accompanying Avis to England. She'll be seeing her grandparents and attending school there."

"Happy to meet you all. Shall we take that walk now, Miss Dolphin? With your permission, of course, Miss Ellis and Miss Smith."

"Of course," says Hilda. "A stroll around the deck will do Avis good. We look forward to hearing more about your island on Wednesday, Professor."

"I look forward to telling everyone about it. Foula is a special place — full of magic and danger."

The professor and I walk in the opposite direction from Hilda and Sarah. As we walk, he tells me about the *Lusy*. He knows everything about boats and ships. He explains:

The *Lusy*'s four giant smokestacks are held up by strong steel wires so they won't topple over. (I'm relieved to hear that.)

The *Lusy* needs 65,000 gallons of water every

minute to keep the engines cool. (Water! Water! Everywhere!)

There are miles and miles of electrical cables running through every part of the ship that keep everything working, from the lights in the dining room to the ice cream machines in the kitchen. (I ask the professor what would happen if one of the cables snaps. He assures me that someone would fix it.)

You'd think that hearing about the insides of a ship and how it works would be boring. But the professor tells it like a story. I can picture everything he describes.

The professor also tells me about his family. His three boys are rambunctious, funny and smart. His wife, Marion, takes care of everything "brilliantly" while he is away speaking and teaching. He adores them all and misses them terribly. He can't wait to see them soon.

As he talks, I feel better and better. Phew! Maybe I am getting my sea legs.

I tell him how much I miss my friend Lizzie and my father and about the small wooden ship he carved for me. "It's my most-prized possession," I tell him. I promise to show it to him.

"I hope you will meet my wife and my boys one day," says the professor. "The boys will drive you crazy with their antics and questions. And if you come to Foula they will show you every nook and cranny on the island."

"I would love to come to Foula," I say. "Is it really magical and dangerous? I hope so. That sounds wonderful."

The professor laughs. "Ah, so you like magic and danger, too. Yes. Foula is surrounded by wild seas and rolling hills that turn emerald green in the summer and deep purple in the fall. Many ships have been wrecked on its jagged rocks. And long ago, they say, Foula was inhabited by a bogeyman and a giant."

We near the bridge to first class, and the professor stops talking about Foula. I really want to hear more, but when the professor says we can explore the first-class section, I'm excited.

"Can we really? Are second-class passengers allowed?" I ask.

"There's only one way to find out," says the professor.

I follow him across the little bridge. No one stops us as we stroll down the thickly carpeted halls. I thought second class was beautiful, but first class is magnificent. Everything is gilded and elegant, especially the passenger elevators.

"Can we ride up?" I ask the professor.

"Why not?"

But before we do, the professor picks up a pamphlet in the purser's office, right beside the elevators. The purser is busy answering passengers' questions. Three people are bombarding him with complaints that the ship is too big and confusing. They've spent an hour hunting for their cabin. Another man complains about a rude steward and how much he hated his eggs at breakfast. "They were horribly dry," he moans so loudly, you'd think they'd served him poison.

The professor and I give each other a look. The poor purser! He tries to be patient, but when a tall, skinny woman wearing a large, floppy hat screams that her room is noisy and "must be changed immediately," the purser starts to sweat and his face and neck turn beet red.

We leave the office and the professor shows me the pamphlet. It's called *The Origins and Issues of the Present War*. "It's been published to convince American passengers that the war is justified," he tells me. "The ship's newspaper is also full of cheerful news about the war and how well it's all going."

He takes a deep breath. He shakes his head as if he's heard terrible news. "So many young men are eager to go to war," he says. "They read the papers and think it will be glorious. But war isn't glorious. It's death, pain and disease. People thought the war would be over in just a few months with easy victories, happy marches and joyful homecomings. But there's no end in sight. There are no easy victories. So many have died already. And not just soldiers. Innocent citizens, too."

I shiver at the professor's words and especially at the pained look on his face. I know he doesn't mean to scare me, but I can't help worrying that this war might come to England, too. What if there is fighting in cities and towns?

My father fought in the Boer War, and the terrible conditions gave him tuberculosis. He died of it. Mother said the Boer War was a nightmare, not just for soldiers and their families, but for thousands of innocent people who lost their homes or were imprisoned or killed.

"Ah, Avis," says the professor. "I've upset you. Here I was taking you for a walk to distract you from your seasickness and I talk of war and I frighten you instead."

"I'm not seasick anymore but I hate thinking about war. I wish there was no war. I wish …"

"I know. Come on. Let's forget about war and ride the elevator!"

The elevator clatters to a stop, and the young operator slides the heavy gilded door open. We step in like we ride first class every day, and the operator bids us good morning. His uniform is as fancy as the elevator. He snaps the door shut, and we rise slowly. I feel like a bird in a beautiful cage.

We step out and stroll down the first-class corridors. We peek into the lounge and the verandah café. Everything glitters and sparkles, from the heavy chandeliers to the gleaming tables and chairs.

"I'd love to see the first-class dining room," I say.

"And so you shall!" says the professor.

We open the first-class dining-room doors. The room has two tiers with a spectacular dome above. The chairs don't swivel like they do in second class but are covered in the softest fabric. There are stately white pillars here, too, and the finest linen napkins and cloths cover each table. (The tables are small and intimate, not long like the tables in second class.)

People linger over breakfast, and a rush of hunger sweeps over me. I ate nothing for breakfast, not even that one piece of toast. If only I could sit down on one of those soft chairs and bite into a warm roll with butter and orange marmalade. But all I can do is watch other people eat.

"There's Mr. Alfred Vanderbilt," whispers the professor. "He's the tall, elegant man with the pink carnation in his buttonhole. He always wears a carnation. He's sitting near Charles Frohman, who produced *Peter Pan* in New York. And those two lovely women are famous actresses. I saw one of them at the theater. Her name is Rita Jolivet."

It isn't polite to stare, but I can't help it. I've never seen a real actress or a play in a theater. It would be exciting to see a play — like seeing a book come to life. I lean forward. I wish I could hear what they're saying. Are they talking about the food, the weather, the war? Have they heard the rumors about U-boats? Are they worried and frightened? I try to guess from their expressions, but all I can see is that they like breakfast. They smile as they spread their toast with thick raspberry jam or orange marmalade, dig into their creamy eggs, smack their lips over a fruity pancake and sip coffee with a touch of cream.

"Mr. Vanderbilt was supposed to sail on the *Titanic* but he decided not to go at the last minute," says the professor. "Lucky man!"

As I glance at Mr. Vanderbilt, a waiter grimaces and waves his hand as if shooing us out. Oh no! We're going to be kicked out of the first-class dining room! I tap the professor on the shoulder. "The waiter is giving us a look. He's coming this way."

We scurry out. As soon as we are safely in the hall we burst out laughing.

"I feel like a spy," I tell the professor. "A first-class spy."

"I wonder what that waiter would have said to us? He probably knows all the first-class passengers by now and we don't look familiar."

"I would have told him that I'm the daughter of a duke, and I missed dinner last night and breakfast this morning because I was seasick," I say. "That's a bit true."

"And a good story," says the professor.

"But I probably wouldn't have been able to say it with a straight face. I'm a terrible liar."

We laugh again. It feels wonderful to laugh.

"The line between storytelling and lying is murky. All storytellers embroider their tales," says the professor.

"What would you have told the waiter?"

"That I am the Laird of Foula, ruler of millions of rocks, at least four hidden caves and deep and treacherous seas. Do you think that would have impressed him?"

"Absolutely! So now please tell me more about Foula and the giant and the bogeyman. What do they look like? What do they do all day on Foula? Do they ever meet people?"

"I can only tell you what I've heard. I've never seen the bogeyman or the giant myself. People say they vanished from Foula many years ago, although my youngest son swears he saw them arguing on the beach on a starlit night. This is what I've heard from people who've lived on the island for years, and they heard it from people who came before them.

"Long, long ago, the bogeyman and the giant were the only two inhabitants of Foula. The bogeyman loved the sea, but he couldn't swim. He only had one good eye but it was so powerful, he could see everything with it.

"The giant towered over the bogeyman, and his voice was louder than thunder. But he was clumsy. He tripped on everything — rocks, seaweed, dead fish.

"The bogeyman and the giant hated each other. They both wanted to be the Laird of Foula. They both craved jewels, coins and gold. Treasure often washed up on the shores of Foula from the ships that smashed against its sharp rocks, and the giant and the bogeyman would hide whatever they found in secret caves.

"Year after year, the bogeyman and the giant quarreled, fought and vied for control of the island. Sometimes the bogeyman had the upper hand. Sometimes the giant triumphed. But neither dominated Foula for long. You'd think they'd have grown tired of their rivalry, but it kept them going.

"That is till the day Jill showed up on Foula. A mermaid helped her to shore. She was twelve years old, the lone survivor of a shipwreck. When the bogeyman and the giant spied Jill on the beach, they were determined to get rid of her. She was the first human girl they had seen in fifty years, and they didn't want her to claim the treasure that had washed up from her ship — a large chest full of gold coins ..."

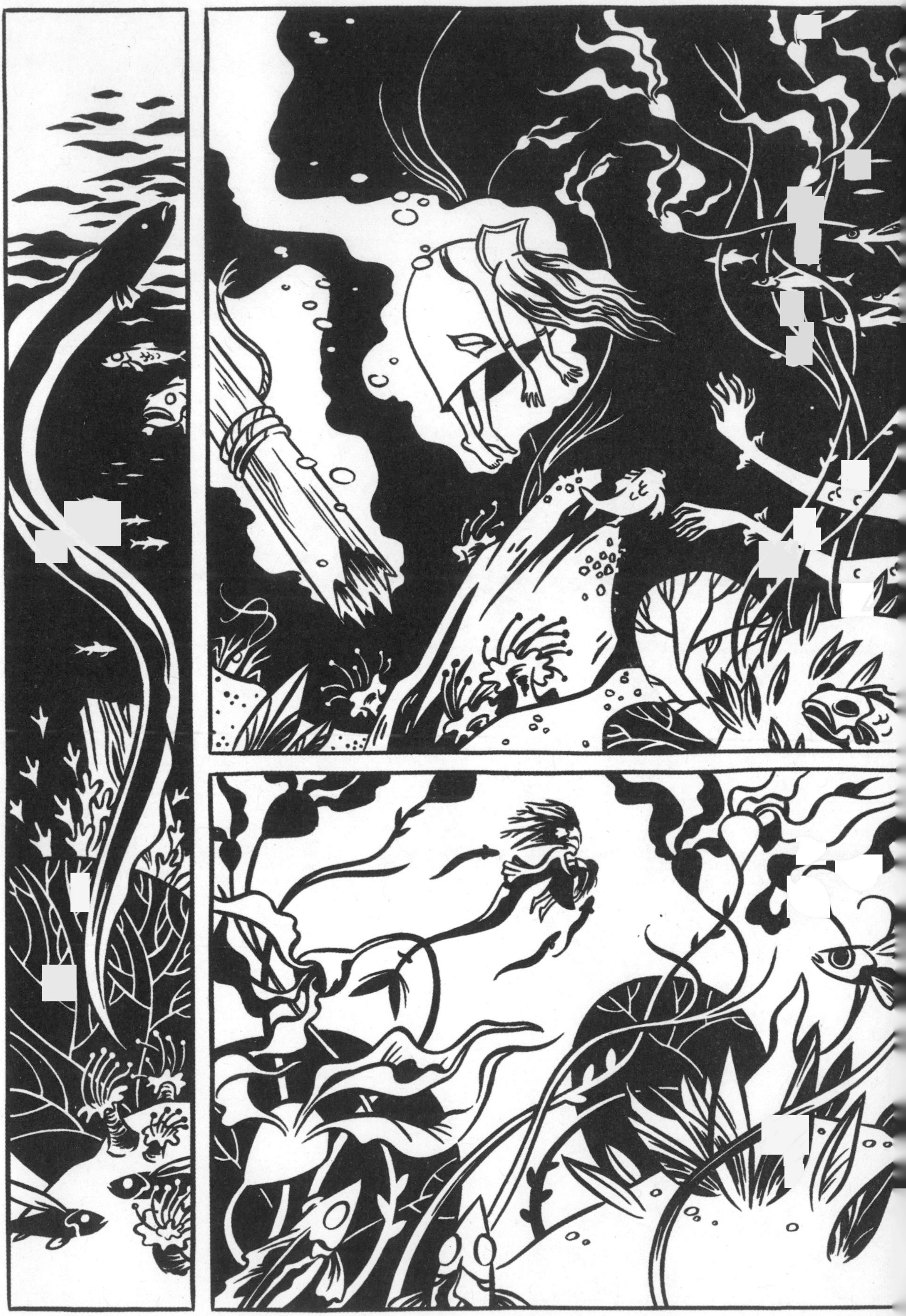

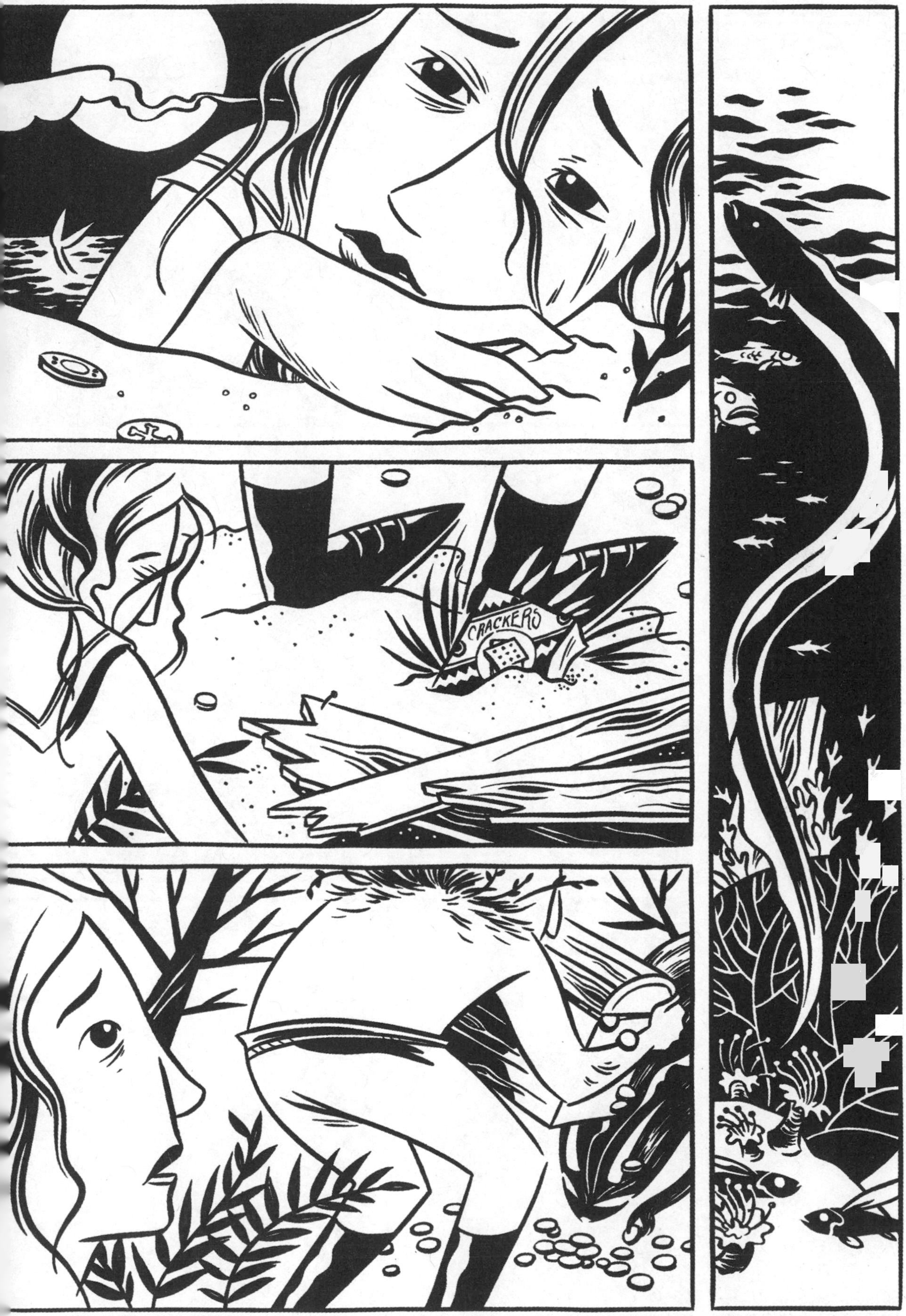
CRACKERS

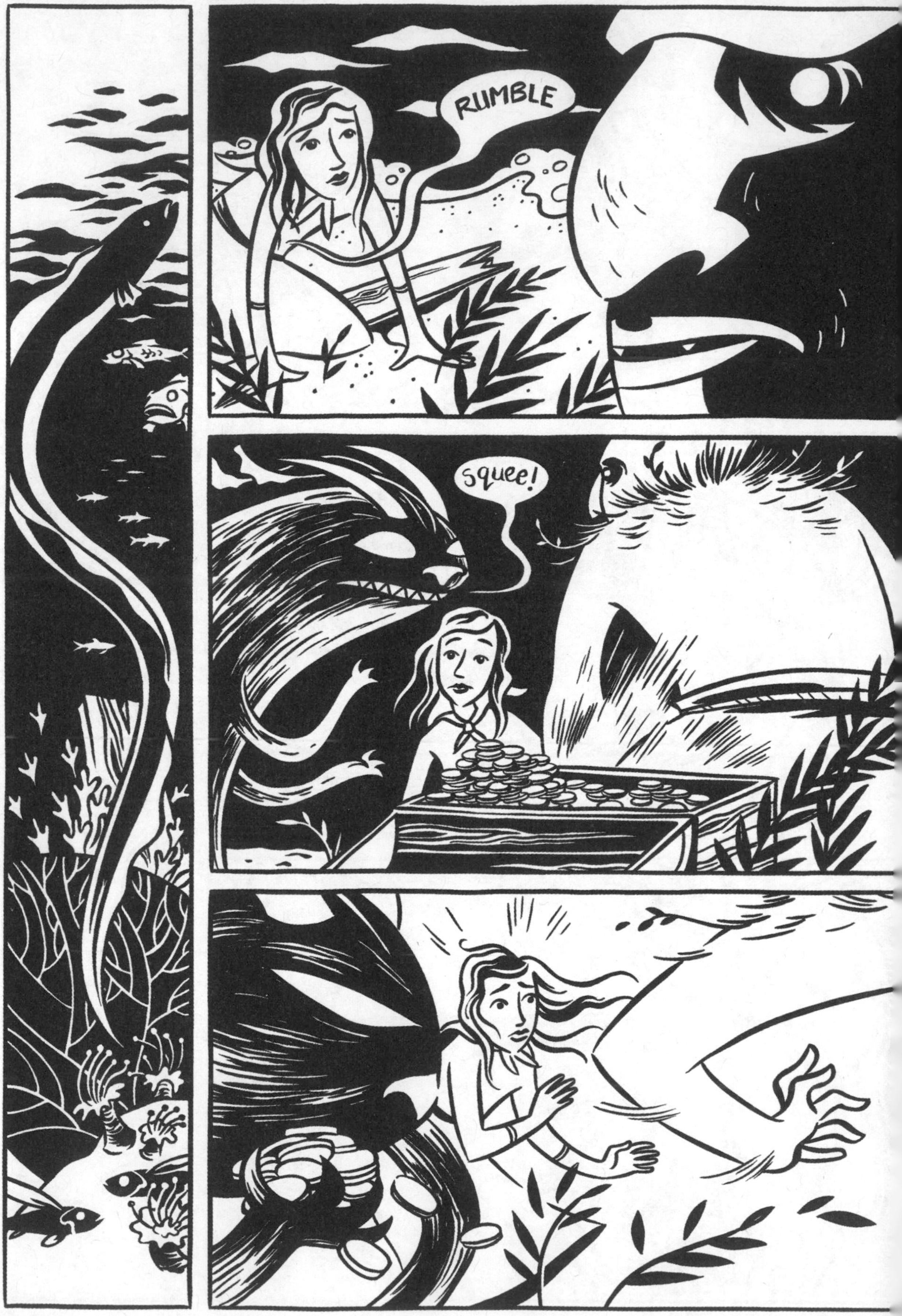
RUMBLE
squee!

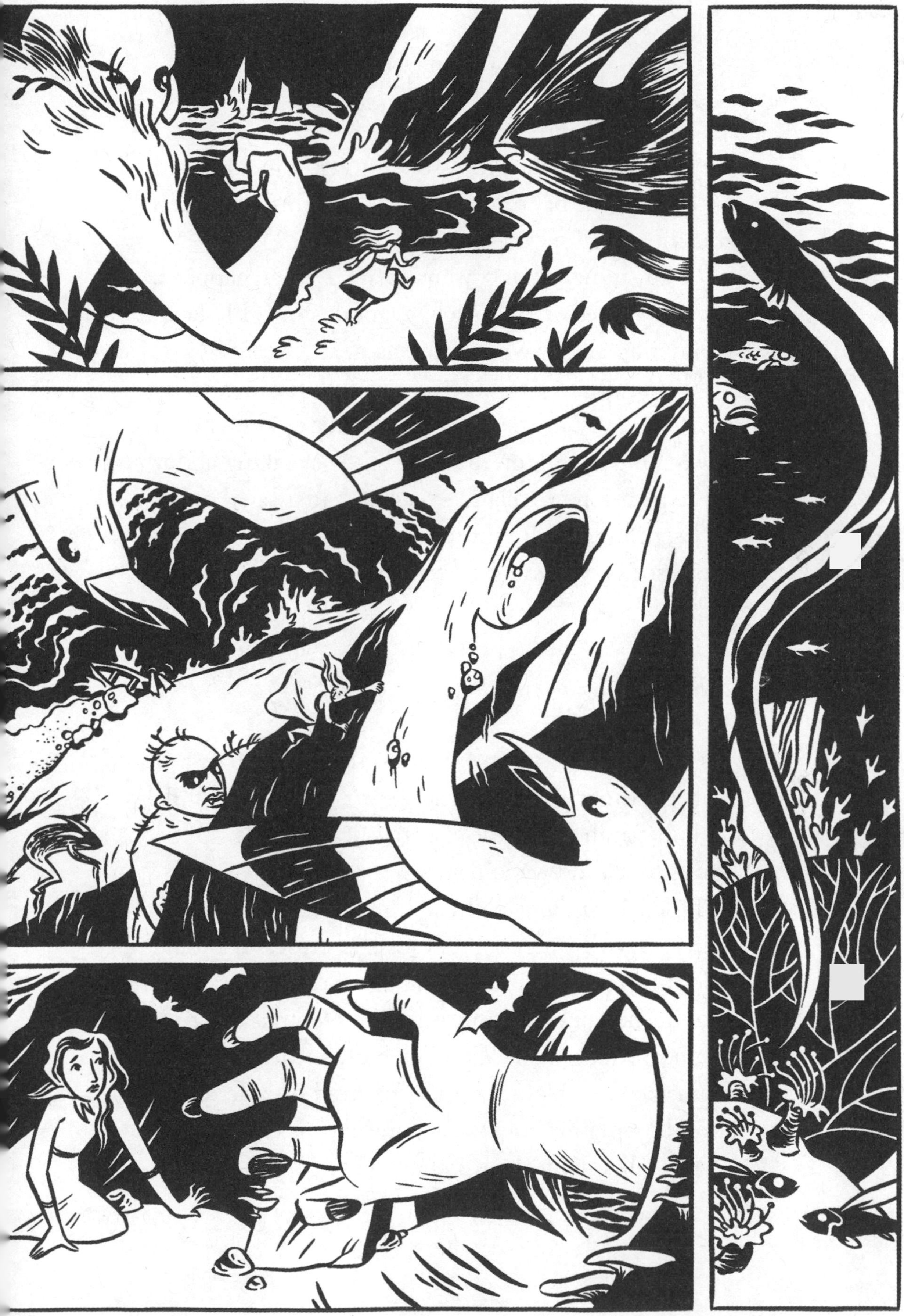

"So what happens next?" I ask.

"Lunch!" says the professor smiling. "I'm famished and you must be, too. I know you didn't eat much this morning."

"I am hungry but I want to hear what happens. Please, Professor. It's such a good story. I'll keep wondering all day what happens next."

"I promise to continue tomorrow morning. Why don't we explore the ship again then? After lunch today I must work on my talk. I'll be speaking about my expedition to Iceland — when I first saw Foula."

I sigh. I can tell by the look on his face that the professor is not going to tell me more about Foula today.

Afternoon • Something Bad

THE PROFESSOR AND I head to the dining room. It feels good not to be seasick. I can't wait to eat. Hilda and Sarah are already seated at our table. Hilda waves to us, and we join them.

Hilda is sipping a thick tomato soup. It smells delicious, so I order some, too. The professor orders cold meats and a salad. Sarah has ordered a pork cutlet, but she's only picking at it. She's too busy talking to a new young man called Peter. He's stocky and has a mustache so black, it looks painted on. He keeps straightening his bow tie as Sarah keeps talking.

She talks about the weather ("Gorgeous, isn't it?"),

the sea ("Have you ever seen anything so blue?"), the food ("Better than the poshest restaurant on shore …") and her cousin Fred ("Poor Fred. He loved the sea till he almost drowned fishing.").

Peter mutters, "Hmm" and "Really?" He looks much more impressed with his food than with Sarah. I wonder if he will ever sit near us again!

After lunch the professor returns to his cabin to work, and Hilda and Sarah stroll back to our cabin to rest. I dash ahead of them, grab my new book and hurry to the lounge.

I can't wait to curl up in a plush chair. It's soft and cozy, like a big nest. I want to kick off my shoes and tuck them under my bottom, but there are too many people around and I'm sure they'd give me a Hilda look if I did.

I read the first chapter of my book. The two main characters, Matt and John, are on the deck of a ship looking at a map and hoping they'll reach the enchanted land soon. They don't know that a pirate ship is about to attack them. They don't know that they are going to have an adventure, but not the one they dreamed of. I am about to turn to chapter two when Sam, the red-haired bellboy, hurries in to deliver messages.

"Did you ever find Dowie?" I ask him.

Sam's freckled face clouds over. "No. Lou and I looked everywhere. Dowie loves the *Lusy* and he loves me and Lou. I know he wouldn't run away unless he thought something bad was going to happen to the ship. I can't stop worrying." Sam swallows and shakes his head. "If something terrible happened, what would I do? I can't swim."

"We're pretty far out," I say. "None of us would make it back to New York from here, even if we can swim."

"I know, and we can't count on being picked up by another ship. It took almost four hours for the *Titanic* survivors to be picked up. Many people died in that dark, icy ocean. I kept thinking about it last night. I hardly slept. Sorry. Don't mean to worry you."

Someone calls Sam's name. He sighs. "I have to go," he says, dashing out of the lounge.

I turn back to my book. But it's hard to read. Sam's words buzz around in my head.

Something bad is going to happen.
Something bad is going to happen.

Evening • A Crazy Symphony

I TOSS AND TURN AGAIN. My head is full of thoughts of home, England, Dowie, Sam, Father, Lizzie, the professor … torpedoes. And to make matters worse, Hilda and Sarah are snoring again. Their snorts and whooshes start and stop. It's like a crazy symphony with everyone hitting the wrong notes. I stuff the ends of my handkerchiefs into my ears, but it doesn't muffle the snoring, and the handkerchiefs keep falling out.

I pick up Father's wooden ship from the basket beside my berth. I stroke it, wishing it was a magic lamp and could bring him back. I miss him so much.

I'm glad I've met the professor. It would be wonderful to visit Foula! I'd watch the waves crash against the rocks, listen to birds, walk along the shore — maybe even meet someone like Jill. And if I did, we'd face the giant and the bogeyman together ...

Day Three
Monday, May 3, 1915

Morning • Ridiculous!

THE SUN STREAMS through my porthole and wakes me up. I open my eyes. Phew! I feel fine — not queasy or dizzy. I crawl to the edge of my berth and peek out. The sky is clear, bright — robin's-egg blue.

And I'm hungry. I hope they have scrambled eggs for breakfast. A plate full of soft, silky eggs would be perfect with hot toast, warm butter and bittersweet marmalade. Maybe the Scottish kind, rich with thick orange bits. We had that once at home and it was so delicious, I crept downstairs at midnight and ate four spoonfuls. I wonder if Professor Holbourn and his family eat marmalade on Foula.

I open the privacy curtains, and there's Hilda washing her face. Sarah is still asleep, whooshing and snorting. I slide off my top berth, and Sarah mumbles something under her breath. It sounds like, "Please, come back. Please …"

I tap her on the shoulder. "Wake up, lazy bones!"

"Who are you calling lazy, Avis?" she grunts. "It's too early to get up."

"It's not early, Sarah," says Hilda. "Breakfast is being served."

Like a bolt of lightning, Sarah tosses off her covers, springs out of bed and grabs her clothes out of the cupboard.

"I told Peter I would see him at breakfast this morning. He'll be so disappointed if I'm not there."

Sarah slips into her clothes before I've even finished getting dressed. Soon we are hurrying down the corridor toward the dining room.

It's noisy and packed with people. Dishes clatter and clang as waiters weave in and out carrying trays piled high with food. Then suddenly a waiter drops a bowl full of oatmeal in a woman's lap. The woman screams and jumps up. The waiter turns white. He apologizes over and over and dashes off for wet towels. His friend brings a broom and rags to wipe up the sticky mess on the floor.

Hilda and I watch it all. Sarah doesn't watch anything. She's too busy hunting for Peter. She searches up and down the long table.

"Oh dear. He probably thinks I stood him up. I must find him. We had such delightful chats yesterday. Then again, maybe he's sleeping in this morning. He's a bookkeeper for a large company in New York. Poor dear. It's exhausting to sit on a chair all day and add up columns of figures. This trip is just the relaxation he needs."

Relaxation? With Sarah talking his ear off? Does Peter really want to see her again? Maybe he's hiding from her. I'd want to hide, especially when she talks on and on. Peter was polite at breakfast and at dinner last night, but he hardly said a word. All he did was nod and eat.

"Let's look for Peter on our walk this morning, Hilda," says Sarah as we sit down at one end of the table.

Hilda's face tightens. She doesn't want to traipse after Sarah on her hunt for Peter. I wouldn't, either.

"You go ahead, Sarah," she says. "I have a headache coming on. I may read after breakfast this morning. I'll join you for lunch."

Sarah gobbles down three pieces of toast and a cup of coffee. Then she scoots off to find Peter before I've even taken a bite of my toast with that wonderful Scottish marmalade. (Yes! They have it!) It's delicious, and so are my scrambled eggs. They're as smooth as silk and as soft as a pillow. Not like the lumpy scrambled eggs Mother makes at home. Mother detests cooking.

"And you, Avis? What will you do this morning?" asks Hilda.

"I'm meeting the professor to explore more of the ship."

"How nice that the professor is paying so much attention to you. He must like children." Hilda dabs a spot of syrup off her face and leaves.

I check the time. Ten minutes before I meet the professor. One more bite of toast and that scrumptious marmalade, and I'm off.

The professor is waiting for me. "How are you feeling this morning?" he asks.

"Much better, although it took forever to fall asleep last night. Hilda and Sarah snored so loudly I was sure the people in first class heard them. I thought someone would bang on our door and demand that they stop. I thought I'd never get to sleep, but then I thought of Foula — the beach, the rocks, the waves and Jill. Foula helped me sleep. Now please tell me what happens next in the story."

"Let's take a look at the lifeboats and I'll tell you on the way. There are enough lifeboats for every passenger on the *Lusitania*, but as far as I know there are no lifeboat drills."

We start to walk. "So, what happened next on Foula, Professor?" I remind him.

"Ah yes," he begins, "the bogeyman and the giant are not pleased to see Jill. They know she saw them eyeing the chest full of gold. They fear someone will try to rescue Jill and discover the gold, and they want the treasure."

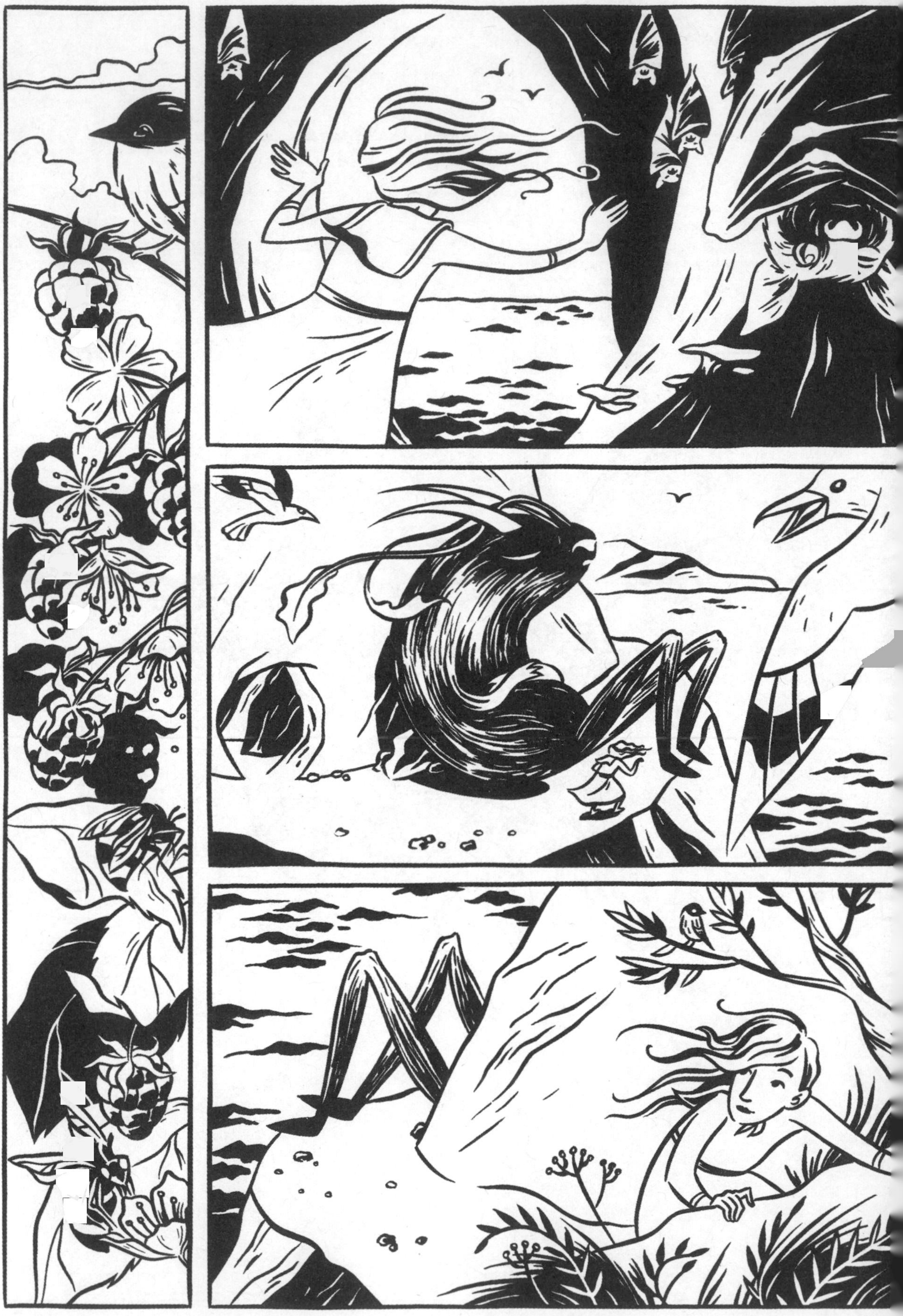

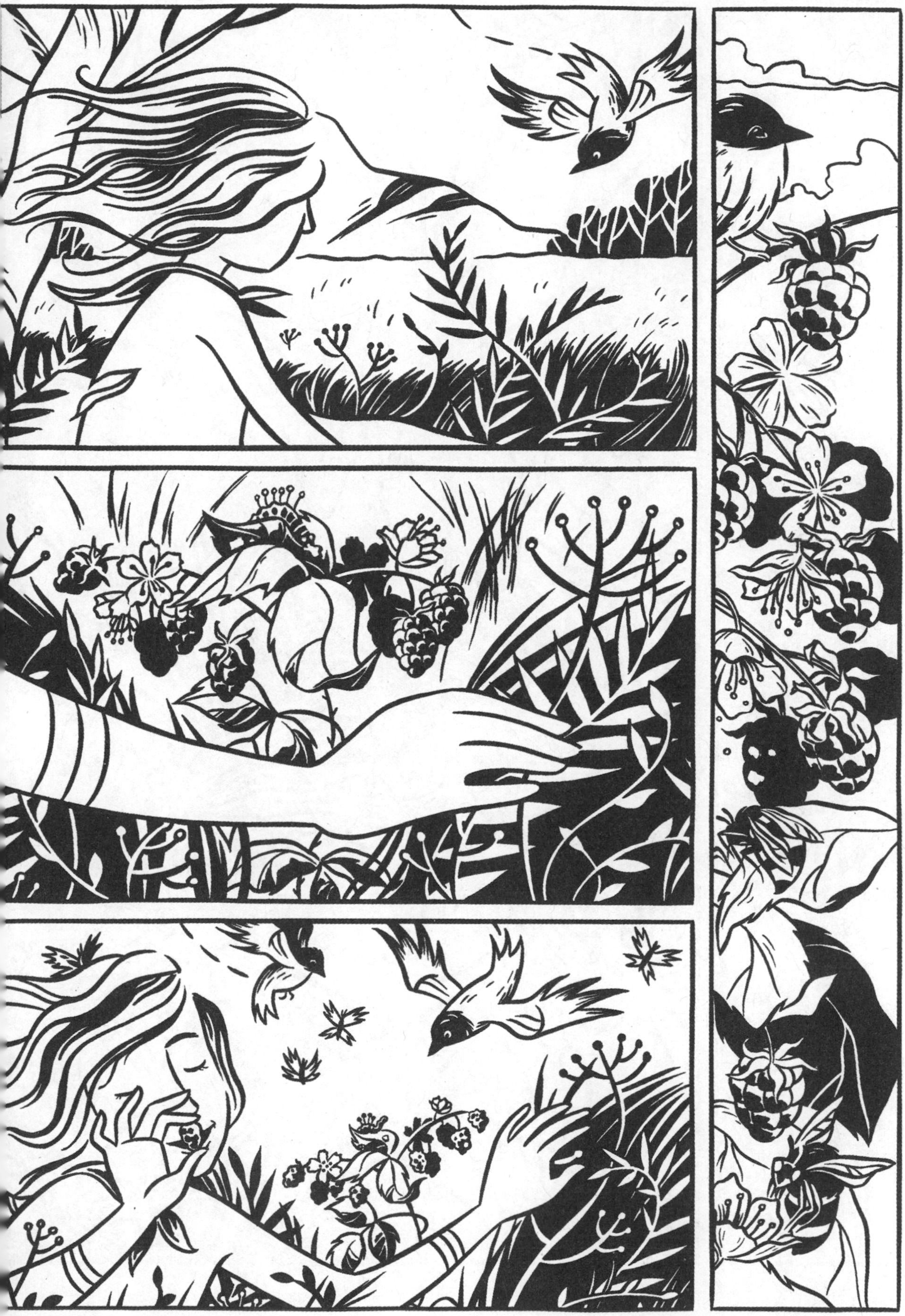

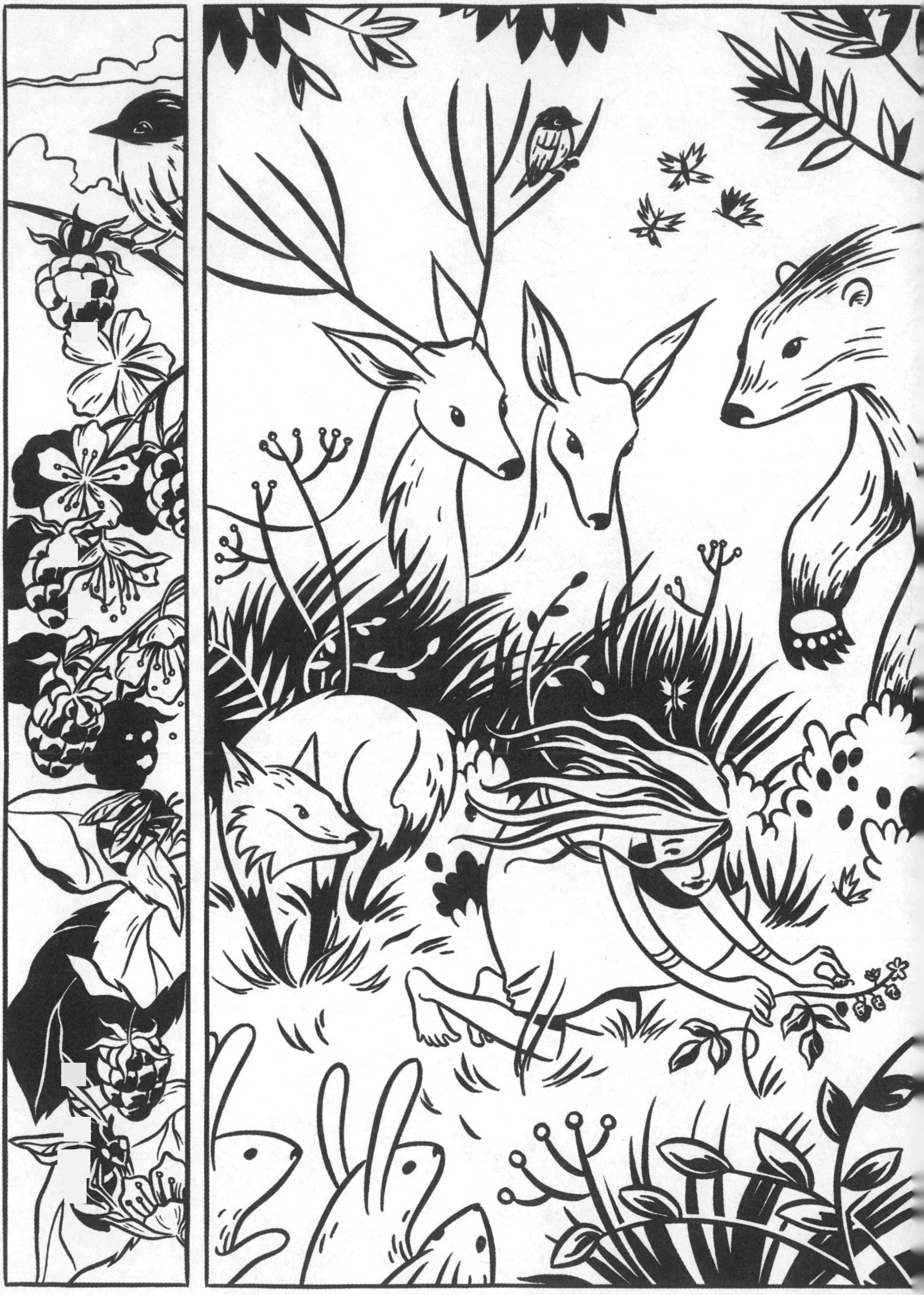

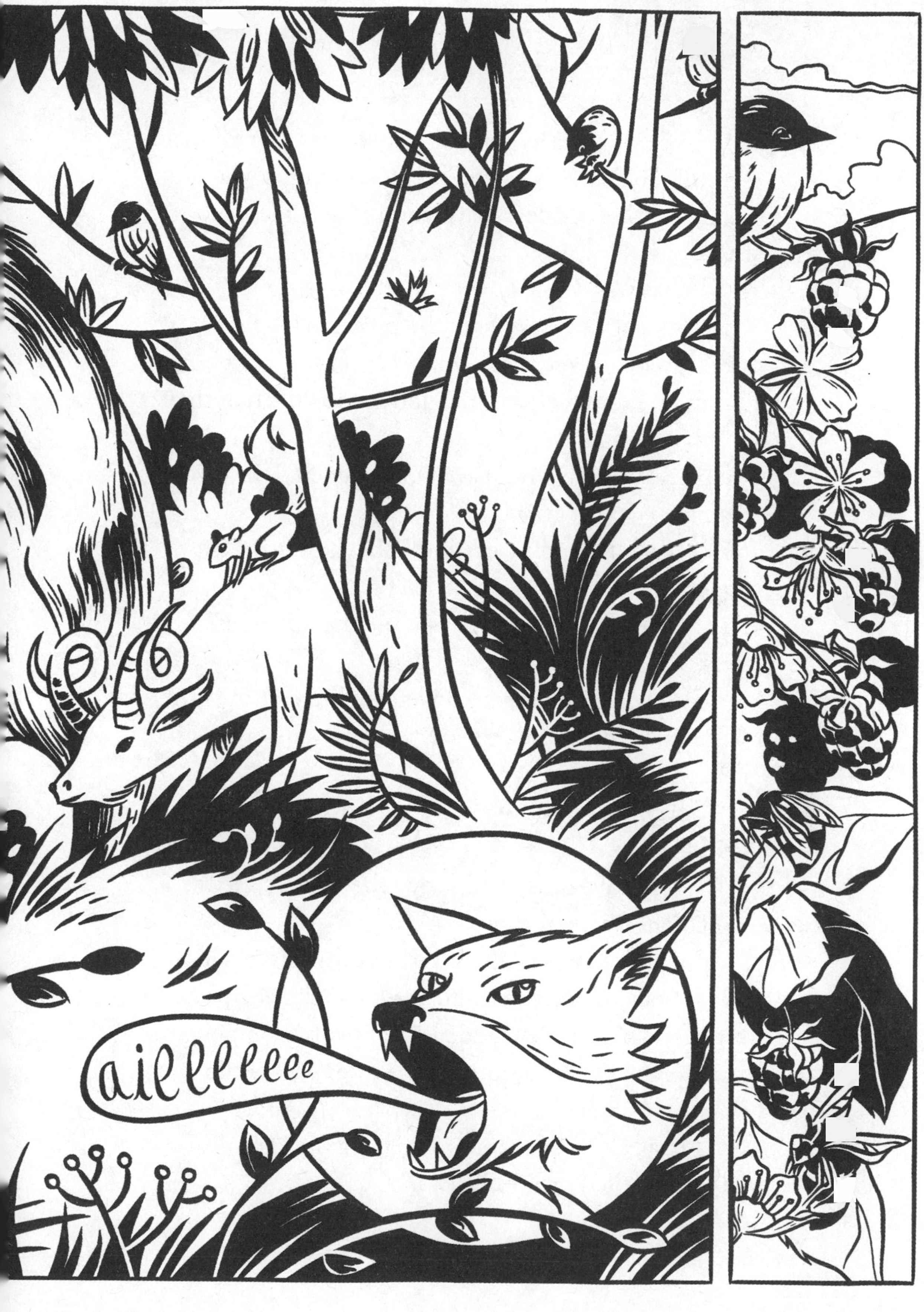
aillllleee

I close my eyes as we near the deck. I can almost see Jill, Foula, the sea, the plants, the birds, the animals … till a sudden sharp sound pulls me back to the *Lusy*.

"What was that?" I ask.

"It's a bugle. Look!" says the professor.

A group of crewmen march over to a lifeboat, climb in, stand for a minute and sit down. Then they climb out again.

Three women and two elderly men join us to watch.

"What's the point of this?" the professor asks a crewman.

The crewman shrugs his shoulders. "Captain's orders, sir."

"Do you know how to lower the lifeboat into the ocean? What procedures are there for passengers in case of an emergency?"

"Sorry, sir, but all we have been told is to do the drill like this."

"Drill! This is no drill," says the professor. "It's a ridiculous waste of time!"

The professor is right. All the crewmen do is jump in and out of a lifeboat. How would that help passengers if something sudden and horrible happened? If the crew doesn't know what to do, how could the passengers know?

"I'll speak to the captain later," says the professor. "This so-called drill is useless."

The crewmen shrug and march away. The small group of passengers whisper to each other. They glance at the professor but say nothing. Then they walk away, too.

"Come on, Avis," says the professor. "Let me show you how a lifeboat works."

The professor and I inspect the lifeboats. Some are all wood, while others have wooden bottoms with collapsible sides. The professor lifts up the canvas cover from one of the collapsible lifeboats and we peek inside.

"You know everything about ships, Professor," I say.

"You know what you love. Ships and the sea are my passion."

They weren't mine till today. I never wondered or cared how a ship was built or how it worked, but the professor makes me care because he cares. I wish he was one of my teachers at school. I might even like mathematics if he taught it!

"Excuse me. Are you Professor Holbourn?"

We look up.

"Captain Turner?" says the professor.

A man in a crisp dark uniform with a sour look on his face glares at us. "I understand you have been interfering with my crew." The captain barks at us like a teacher whose students have misbehaved. He looks like he wants to send us both to stand in the corner.

But his brusque manner doesn't rattle the professor. "We have not been interfering with anything, Captain," he says. "I have some concerns I was hoping to broach with you later today."

"What kind of concerns?" The captain shoots his words out like a gun.

"When will you have lifeboat drills for the passengers?" asks the professor.

"There will be no lifeboat drills. They are unnecessary. It would only upset the passengers."

"I disagree," says the professor.

Captain Turner's eyes narrow. "Are you telling me how to run my ship?" he bellows.

"No. I am simply suggesting something I feel would benefit everyone aboard. We must be prepared for any possibility, especially in times of war, Captain."

"How dare you, sir. You are obviously frightening this young woman and I will not have you frighten any other passengers aboard my ship. They are my responsibility and you are interfering with that, sir."

"Professor Holbourn isn't frightening me," I tell the captain. "He's trying to help us."

The captain gives me a look. It's like one of Hilda's looks, but angrier. Then he turns on his heels and stomps off.

"Why won't he listen?" I say.

"Clearly, the captain isn't fond of anyone disagreeing with him. But one thing he said may be true. I worry that I've frightened you, Avis, and I don't mean to do that. I just want us to be prepared."

"I am a little frightened but I'm trying not to be. Being scared doesn't help."

"But being prepared does. And being scared is natural. At least there are lifebelts on board for each passenger, but I'm sure few people bother to learn how to put them on. And they're clumsy. You don't have time to figure out how to put a lifebelt on in an emergency. You can't fumble."

"I haven't even seen my lifebelt. I'll look for it in my cabin and try it on as soon as I go back."

"Good. And promise me, Avis, if anything happens, you'll find me."

I nod, but my heart pounds at his words. I know the professor doesn't want to scare me, but it's hard not to be afraid.

"I promise I'll look for you, Professor, but nothing will happen. It can't. Everyone says the ship can outrun any German U-boat. That's true, isn't it?"

The professor pats me gently on the back. "The *Lusitania* is fast and strong. The British Admiralty are aware of our movements. I'm just cautious, despite my love of magic and danger."

The professor winks. I wink back.

"It's strange," I say, "but I can only wink with my left eye."

"And I can only wink with my right! We are a perfect team, Avis. Now, I'm hungry. All this arguing with the captain has given me a fierce appetite."

We walk along the deck and stop at the railing to look out to sea. The sun glitters on the water. The sea is calm and as blue as the sky. It's like we're gliding on glass. I can't imagine anything terrible happening on a day like today. The ship feels strong and steady, although it still sways a little. But my stomach must be getting used to it.

"Hello, Avis."

I turn around. It's Sarah, her arm hooked in Peter's. She looks as pleased as if she just landed a giant fish.

"You remember Avis, Peter," she says. "I'm her guardian on this trip. You met at dinner last night."

Peter nods. "Good to see you again," he mumbles.

"But I don't think you've met Professor Ian Holbourn, our famous writer and the Laird of the Isle of Foula. The professor will be speaking about his expedition to Iceland on Wednesday. We are looking forward to his talk."

Peter nods again. "Nice to meet you, Professor," he mutters.

"Well, we'll be going then," says Sarah. She tightens her grip on Peter's arm. "See you at lunch, Avis."

Sarah and Peter walk on. I can hear her telling Peter more about Professor Holbourn. She's talking about him as if he's a world-famous celebrity and one of her best friends.

"It looks like Miss Smith has found a beau," says the professor.

"I'm not sure he likes being found," I say.

"He didn't look too unhappy to me."

I make a face. "Really? Sarah would drive me crazy if I were her beau but she said Peter is a bookkeeper. Maybe it's nice to hear someone talk all the time if all you do all day is sit on a stool adding up numbers."

The professor laughs. "You are probably right, Avis."

As soon as we enter the dining room, Hilda waves to us. We head over and she introduces us to her new friends, Jane and her brother, Richard. Jane is tall and as thin as a stick, and so is Richard. They look like twins, and it turns out they are. I've never met adult twins before. They both talk a mile a minute, although Jane talks a little bit faster than Richard. Hilda's eyes bounce back and forth between them like she's watching a tennis game. I think she likes Richard more than Jane. Her smile is wider and warmer when she listens to him.

"Avis is in my charge," she says, and then she introduces the professor as if he were *her* best friend. Everyone is impressed that the professor is a writer and the Laird of Foula.

Sarah sits across the table with Peter. She takes tiny, delicate bites of her food and sips her tea with her pinky in the air as if she's a duchess. Peter wolfs down his boiled mutton and nods at everything she says. I hate mutton. I don't know how anyone can eat it, especially when it's boiled, but Peter smacks his lips over every bite.

My chicken soup with thick noodles is delicious. And my apricot tart is the best dessert I've ever had. That may be because Mother's idea of dessert is a cake she calls "sponge." It tastes like a sponge with all the water wrung out.

The professor has vegetable soup, a salad and sago pudding for dessert. Sago, he explains, is a plant that comes from Asia. "This pudding is good," he says, "but nothing compares to my wife's desserts. Marion is an artist with desserts."

I liked Marion before, but now I like her even more! I can't wait to meet her. The professor invites me to visit them soon after we land. I'm glad that I know someone in Scotland. Someone kind and funny. I know that Foula is way up north, but I'm going to visit the professor there. No matter what!

After lunch the professor and I leave the dining room together. He's returning to his cabin to work on his talk. I'm going to read in the lounge again. But before we get very far, three men march over to us. They look like they're about to explode.

"Are you Professor Holbourn?" barks one of the men. His stomach sticks out so much, it almost touches the professor.

"I am," says the professor.

"We insist that you stop discussing lifeboats and drills. My wife and her friend were needlessly alarmed by your remarks this morning. We spoke to Captain Turner and he was furious with you — as we are."

"You are upsetting the passengers, especially the ladies," says one of the other men. He's short and bald, but his voice is so loud, I'm sure everyone in the dining room can hear him.

"I'm sorry that your wife and her friend are upset," says the professor, "but I'm concerned for all our safety. We need lifeboat drills and our captain doesn't see it that way."

"He's the captain, not you!" says the stocky man with the huge stomach. He points, and for a minute I'm sure he's going to drill his finger into the professor's chest.

But the professor doesn't flinch. "You are entitled to your opinion, gentlemen, and I am entitled to mine," he says. "But I would think carefully about discouraging our captain from doing what is sensible and right. Good day."

The men stomp away. They are just as angry as when they charged over to lecture the professor.

"There goes the Ostrich Club," he says.

"Ostrich Club? What do you mean?" I ask.

"Ostriches stick their heads in the sand when there's danger. They imagine that hiding from danger will make it disappear. But it never does. I'm not saying that we're in danger on the *Lusitania*. I'm only saying we should be prepared."

"I'm definitely going to check my lifebelt as soon as I return to my cabin."

The professor pats me on the back. "We'll be fine, Avis. Please don't worry. Now I'm off to prepare for my talk. I'll see you for a walk tomorrow after breakfast. Same time. Same chair. There's lots more to see on this ship!"

"And lots more to hear about Foula," I remind him. "I can't stop thinking about Jill. What will the giant and the bogeyman do to her? How will she escape? How will she survive?"

"Poor Jill. She must fend for herself. But I have faith in her. She'll find a way." The professor winks with his right eye.

I wink with my left.

When I get back to my cabin, I see the lifebelt immediately. It's on top of the closet. I climb up to my bunk, lean over and yank it down. It's big and bulky, but I struggle into it.

I gaze at myself in the mirror and wince. I look like a big, overstuffed bear. The door opens and Hilda comes in.

"Good heavens, Avis! What are you doing?"

"The professor thinks we should practice putting on our lifebelts. You should try yours on, too."

Hilda rolls her eyes. "I will do no such thing. You're thinking too much again and worrying for nothing. I'm surprised the professor encourages you. There will be no need for lifebelts on this voyage. And that contraption makes you look ridiculous. I must go. I only came back to get my cape. It's chilly outside, and Jane and Richard and I are going for a stroll."

I shove the lifebelt back on top of the closet. I hope Hilda is right, and the professor is just being cautious.

I grab my book and head for the lounge. I snuggle into a big chair. Matt and John have just spied the pirate ship. They're terrified but also excited. Can they fight off the pirates? Before I find out, Sam the bellboy scoots over.

"Good book?" he asks.

"Really good. Any sign of Dowie?"

"No sign anywhere. I miss that cat. I wonder if I'll ever see him again."

We both sigh. I know we're thinking the same thing.

We're one day closer to England.

One day closer to shore, and to danger, because German U-boats lurk near the coast.

Day Four
Tuesday, May 4, 1915

Morning • Pots, Pans and Giants

THE SUN WAKES me again. Another blue-sky morning! I leap out of bed. I'm dressed even before Hilda and Sarah budge from their berths.

"You're up early, Avis. How nice," says Hilda, sitting up. "I'm pleased you've taken my advice and are enjoying the trip."

"I am having a good time, Hilda," I say. "I like exploring with the professor."

"Yes, he has been kind to take you under his wing. You are a lucky young lady."

I *am* lucky that I met the professor. And Hilda and Sarah are lucky, too. They don't have to think or worry about me. They can flirt all they want with their new beaus, Peter and Richard.

Hilda is up and dressed now. "So where are you going today?" she asks while sticking pins into her hair.

"I want to see the galley where they prepare all the food."

"How nice," says Sarah, stretching her arms and yawning.

"Are you meeting Peter again?" I ask her.

"Of course. We have become good friends. So Hilda, will you be seeing Jane and her brother, Randolph? Or is it Rupert — or Ronald?"

"Richard," snaps Hilda as she slips into her dress. "Yes. I intend to see them. We share many interests. They enjoy music and we hope to attend the concerts on board. They love to travel and have already visited Italy, France and India. They even rode on an elephant."

"Really? But they speak so quickly," says Sarah. "It's a wonder you understand a word."

I stare at Sarah. Why does she have a triumphant look on her face? Why is she sniping at Hilda? It's like they're rivals for the same boyfriend, but I know they're not.

Hilda gives Sarah one of her looks. "I have no trouble understanding them. They are delightful companions. Your friend Peter doesn't speak much, does he?"

Hilda and Sarah's conversation is becoming stranger by the minute. They were getting along fine till this morning. What's happened between them?

"Peter is a quiet man. A deep thinker. I like that about him," says Sarah, primping her curls.

"I'm sure he is … deep," says Hilda. She pats her hair and smoothes her long blue skirt.

By now we are all dressed. I'm dying to know

what's going on between Sarah and Hilda, but I can't ask, of course. We walk in silence to the dining room. As soon as we arrive, Hilda rushes over to sit beside Jane and Richard.

Sarah scours the room for Peter, but he's nowhere in sight. "He must be sleeping in, the poor dear. We were up till almost midnight talking in the lounge," she says. "Hilda was furious when I came in. She complained that I woke her. Is it my fault she's a light sleeper? Come on, Avis. Sit near me."

Could that be it? Did Hilda bark at Sarah, and Sarah resents her for it? No. There must be more to it than that. Sarah and I sit at the opposite end of the table from Hilda. Sarah keeps checking the room as the waiter takes our order.

"Oh, just three pieces of toast," says Sarah, "and the oatmeal. And a few pancakes with syrup."

I order scrambled eggs again, with toast and hot chocolate.

"Hilda has become so difficult," says Sarah. "I think she's jealous of my friendship with Peter. She only met Jane and her brother, Randolph or Rupert or whatever his name is, yesterday."

"Richard," I tell her.

"Yes. Richard. Between you and me, Avis, I think Hilda is smitten with Richard but it's obvious he's not interested in her. He just likes to talk."

I stifle a laugh. Sarah likes to talk just as much as Jane and Richard.

"Oh! There's Peter," she says.

Sarah bolts from her seat and waves at him. He shuffles over, smiles a tight little smile and sits down beside us. Sarah looks up and tries to catch Hilda's eye. I know she wants Hilda to notice that Peter is sitting beside her. But Hilda's eyes are glued to Richard and Jane.

"I'm so sorry I kept you up so late last night," Sarah coos at Peter. "But wasn't it lovely to chat?"

Peter nods and orders breakfast. Eggs, pancakes, bacon, hominy grits, toast, syrup and coffee.

For the rest of breakfast, Sarah nibbles at her food and talks. Peter digs into his breakfast like it's his last meal on earth. He only looks up from his plate to mumble, "Yes" or "That's interesting" or "Very nice." He's happy to wolf down a mountain of food and listen to Sarah.

But I'm not! As soon as I finish my eggs and toast, I escape.

"Have a nice morning, Avis!" Sarah sings out as I dash out of the dining room.

The professor is waiting for me beside "my" chair — the one on the deck where we first met and where we meet every day now.

"Where shall we explore?" asks the professor.

"How about the galley? I love kitchens. My mother owns a nursing home and I always pop into the kitchen to see what's cooking or baking — unless my mother is cooking. She's a terrible cook and an even worse baker."

The professor laughs. "I can see that you and my wife, Marion, will get along famously. She loves to cook and bake." The professor pats his stomach. "I love to eat her results."

I laugh. "I bet the *Lusy*'s kitchens are amazing. Their pots and pans must be enormous. Big enough for a giant like the one on Foula."

"I take the hint, Avis. And I haven't forgotten. I promise to tell you what happened next on Foula after we explore."

We head down the stairs to the shelter deck, but before we get very far we stop. Six crewmen lead three men past us. The men's hands are tied tight behind their backs, like prisoners.

"What's going on?" the professor asks.

"We discovered these stowaways in the steward's pantry, sir. We suspect they're German spies."

I shiver. "Spies? Spies on the *Lusy*?"

"Don't worry, miss. Detective Inspector Pierpoint will interrogate the prisoners," says the sailor. "We caught these three in time. No harm was done."

I glance at the stowaways. Two are middle-aged, and they stare straight ahead as if they see nothing and no one. But the third stowaway is younger. He can't be more than twenty years old.

"Move!" the sailors shout at the men.

The stowaways shuffle along the deck, but before they reach the stairs the young man turns and looks at me. His brown eyes are wide with fear. He doesn't look like a spy. He looks terrified, like a kid who's in trouble and doesn't know how to get out of it. Maybe he's not a spy, or maybe he was forced to become a spy, or maybe he's poor and had to hide on the *Lusitania* because he didn't have enough money to pay for his passage home to Germany.

People in Canada and the United States hate Germans since the war broke out. Everyone is suspicious and angry. A week before I left home, Mrs. Baumgarten, who lives next door to us and was born in Germany, was taunted and even spat on. And all she did was buy potatoes at the store. That night someone threw a rock through her window. She ran over to our house, shaking and crying. "I have done nothing to hurt anyone," she sobbed. "Why do they want to hurt me?" Mother held her hand and made her a cup of tea. But all Mother could say was, "It's not you, Margaret. It's the war."

I tell the professor what I'm thinking as we walk to the galley.

"You might be right, Avis. That young fellow doesn't look like a spy to me, either. But it's difficult to know, especially in wartime. Rumors fly like leaves in the wind."

We open the galley door. The cooks are wearing checked trousers and white shirts. I ask a tall, blond cook if we can come inside.

"It's tight in here and we're preparing lunch," he says. "But you're welcome if you can find room."

He's right! The space is so tiny and cramped, it's amazing that so many people can rush back and forth with arms full of food, plates, pots, pans and trays without getting burned or knocked to the floor. The kitchen staff wiggle around each other, slicing, cooking, mixing, baking and arranging food on each plate. And somehow, magically, everything that comes out is perfect and beautiful.

The galley staff work so hard and so fast. We just had breakfast, and they're busy preparing lunch already! Lovely smells fill the small space — meat, cheese, onions, puddings and cakes.

"I read," says the professor, "that in a typical crossing 130 pigs, 80 sheep, 10 calves, 60 lambs, 150 turkeys, 90 geese, 20 pheasants and 400 pigeons are needed to stock the pantry. And that's just the beginning. Imagine the towers of fruit and vegetables, cream, butter, cheese and milk."

"And most important of all — chocolate. I love chocolate." I point to a mound of it piled high in a corner. "I can't believe that the ship doesn't sink with all the food, people and furniture."

"No, that won't sink her," says the professor laughing. "The *Lusitania* can handle the weight."

"Excuse me. Excuse me," says a cook, his arms piled up to his nose with cauliflower and broccoli.

"Could you move to the side, miss?" says a waiter carrying six trays of dirty breakfast dishes.

The waiters move like acrobats at the circus. They

balance trays and squeeze and shimmy between chairs, tables and people. As I hug the wall to let one waiter pass, another waiter with three trays overloaded with bread, butter and salt and pepper shakers steps on my foot.

"Ouch!"

"Sorry, miss," he says. "Are you hurt?"

"A little, but I'll be fine."

"Let's go, Avis," says the professor, "before they toss us out."

I limp out behind him and sit on the first chair we see. I slip off my shoes. I can wiggle my toes, so my foot isn't broken but it's definitely sore.

"Are you able to walk?"

"Kind of."

"Do you mind if we take a look at the lifeboat drills again?" asks the professor.

"Sure. Only one foot hurts. The other one's fine."

The professor laughs. "Good! Nothing stops you, Avis Dolphin. Not even squashed toes."

"And nothing stops you, Professor Holbourn. Not even a stubborn, grumpy captain." I know that the professor still hopes he can persuade the captain to organize proper lifeboat drills for the passengers. "You promised to tell me what happens next with Jill on Foula," I remind him as we walk.

"Ah yes, where did we leave Jill?"

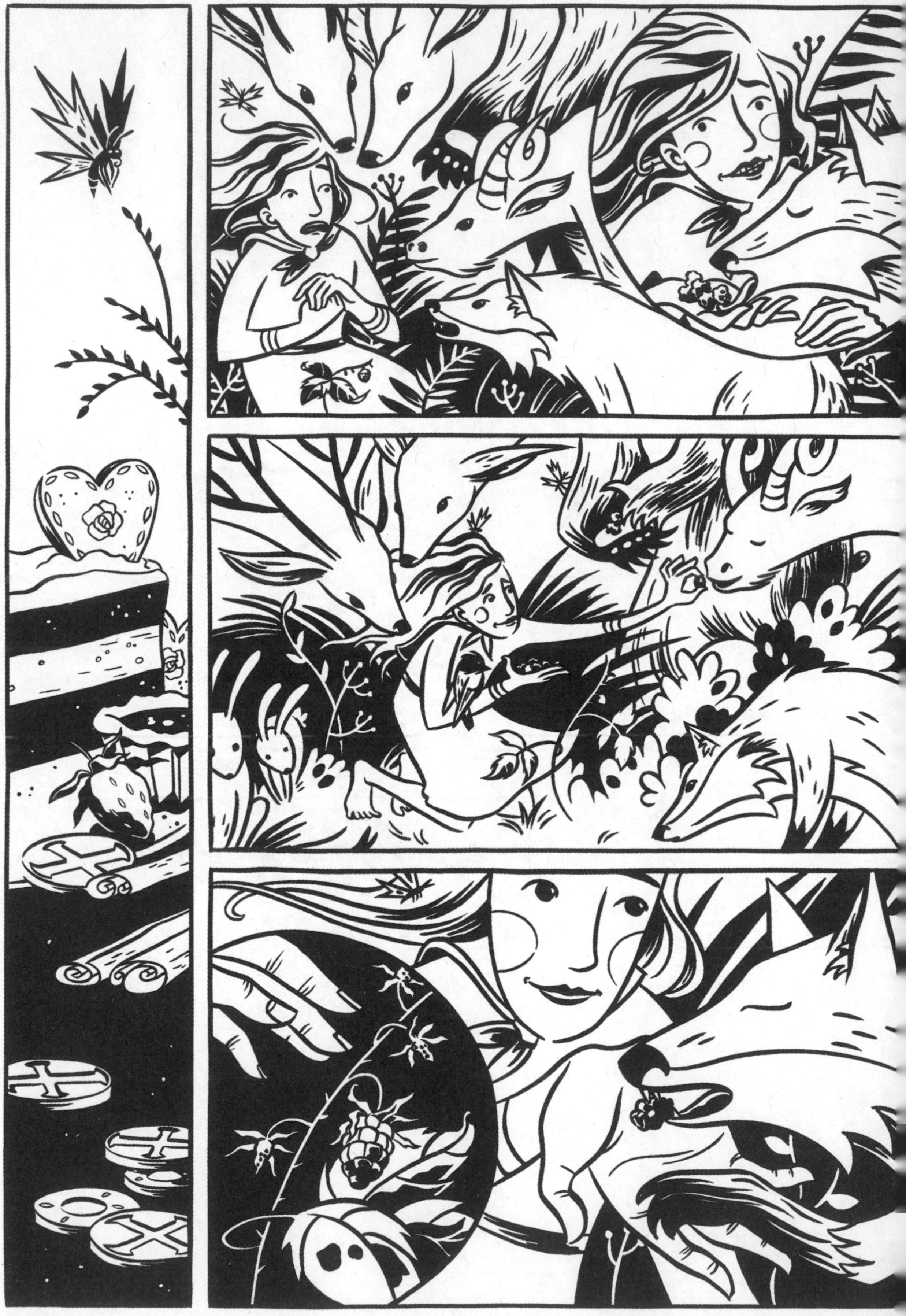

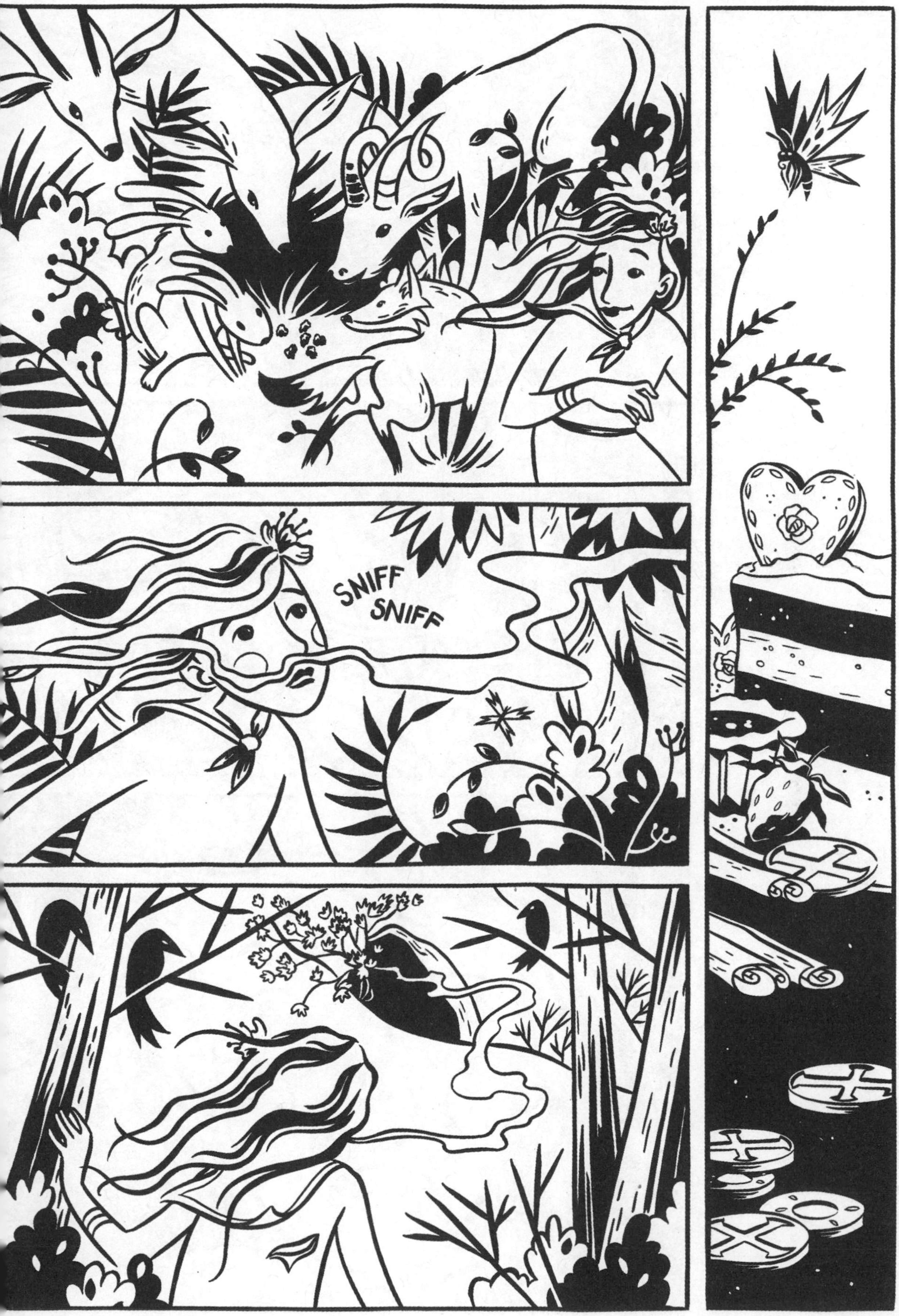
SNIFF
SNIFF

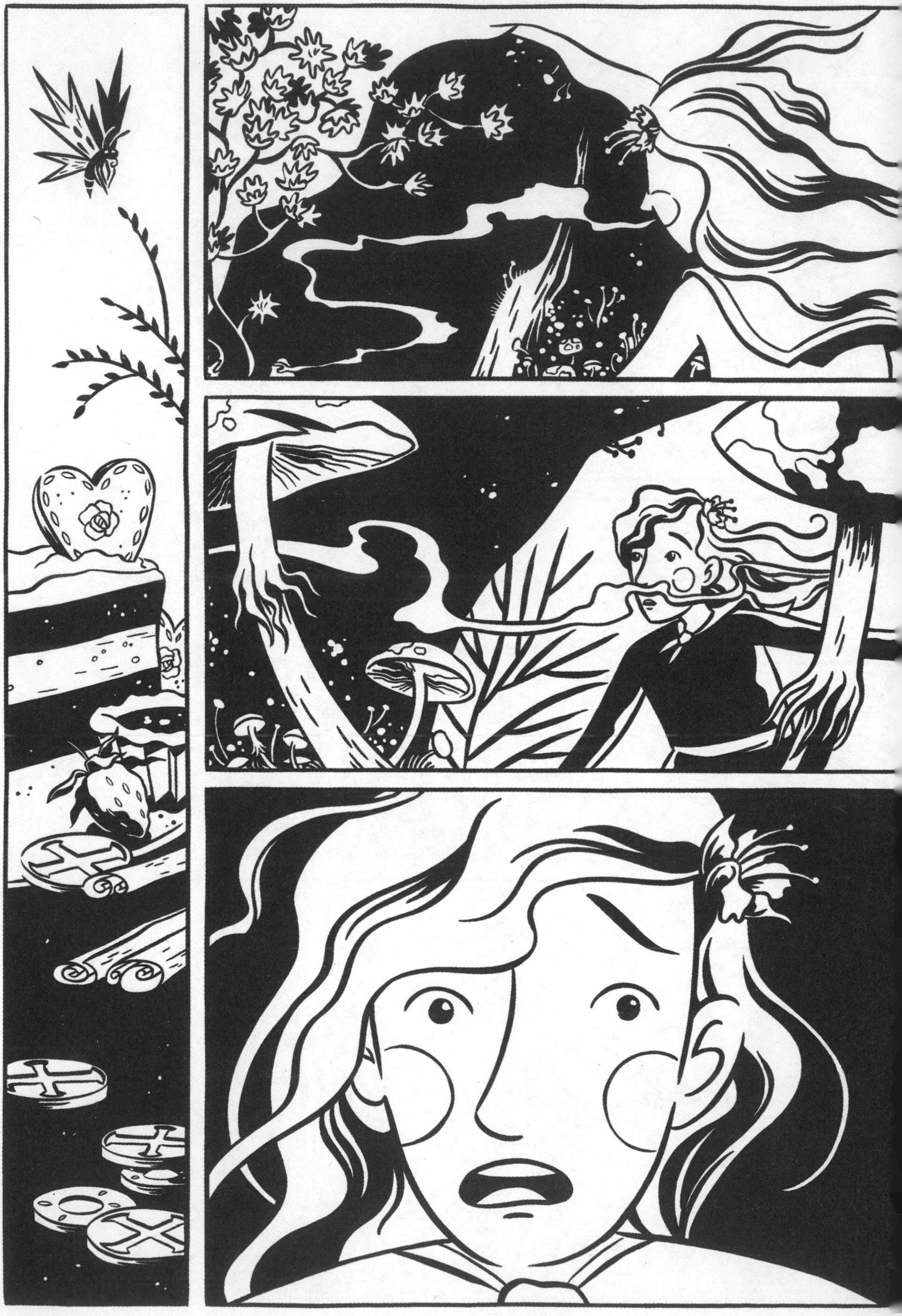

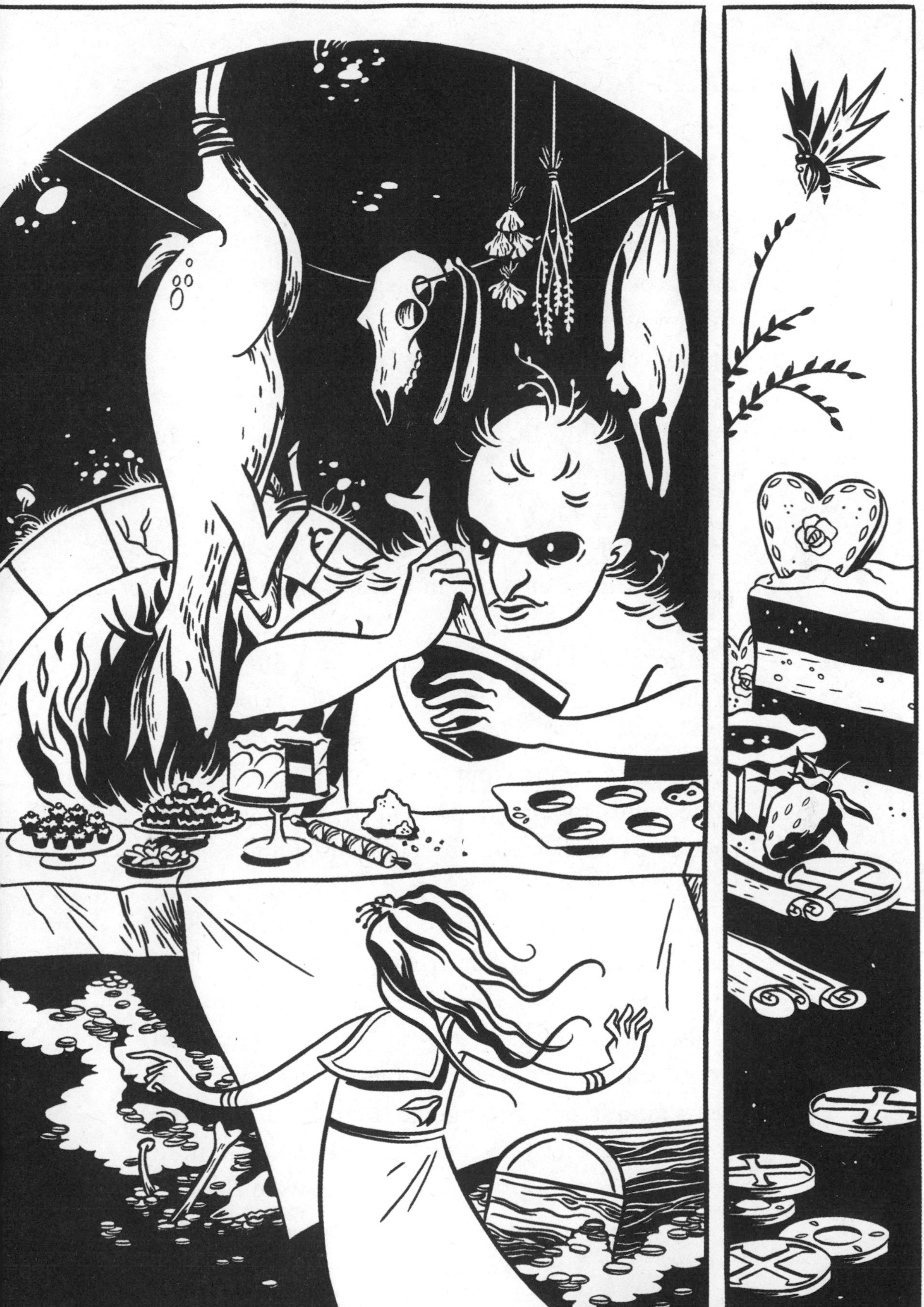

"Oh, Professor!" What will Jill do now?"

Before he can answer, there's a rustling sound, followed by a thud. Someone is sliding against the side of a lifeboat. We draw closer and peer down. The canvas cover is wrinkled. People are in there.

"Stowaways?" I whisper to the professor. "Or spies with knives or guns?" I back away.

The professor shakes his head. "I don't think spies would hide in the lifeboat. It's too easy to get caught with the daily drills."

Another thud.

"Who's in there?" I whisper.

"I think there are birds in there," says the professor.

"Birds? What kind of birds?"

The professor raises his eyebrows. "Lovebirds."

"Are you sure?"

"I heard a rumor about this. Watch."

He points to two crewmen approaching the lifeboat. One marches over and raps on the hull.

"Out!" he barks.

The lifeboat canvas pops up, and a man and woman peek out from inside. The young woman's hair hangs like a dishrag. The man's hair stands up like he just got out of bed. They smooth their rumpled clothes and tamp down their messed-up hair. Then they scramble out. I recognize them both from the dining room. They were sitting together yesterday, so deep in conversation, you'd think they were alone in that big, noisy room. Now the woman's face is bright red, and so is her neck. The man has giant sweat circles under his armpits, staining his pale blue shirt.

"Sorry," they mutter. They scurry off like rabbits.

"This happens at least once a day," says the crewman. "It happened three times yesterday. I couldn't believe it. I found three couples in there, one after another."

"It's not a lifeboat. It's a love boat," I say.

As soon as the words slip out of my mouth, a man elbows his friend and guffaws. A woman gives me a Hilda look. Oh no! I know what they think! The couples in the lifeboat might be doing more than hugging and kissing.

I imagine Sarah and Peter in the lifeboat. Sarah would love cuddling in there, but Peter wouldn't — unless, of course, they served food. As for Hilda and Richard, Hilda would never let her perfect hair get messed up like that.

"You need a sign. No smooching in the lifeboats," I tell the crew.

"Good idea, miss. I'll take it up with the captain." The crewman bites his lip. I can tell he's trying not to laugh.

Soon the two crewmen are joined by three more and a small group of passengers. We watch the crew do their lifeboat drill again. The professor and I look at each other. I know we're thinking the same thing. This drill looks even more useless the second time.

And we're not the only ones who think that.

"What's the point of this?" asks a woman in a blue feathered hat. "Why do they bother?"

"I agree," says the professor. "We have to be prepared properly for a real emergency, especially now that we're nearing shore."

"Oh dear! Do you think we could be torpedoed, Professor?" asks a woman in a black hat. She squeezes her husband's arm.

"Cut that out, Wanda! And stop worrying," snaps her husband. He pushes her arm away. "The captain reassured us. We're fine. Absolutely fine."

"I hope so," says the professor.

Afternoon • Triumph and Tears

WHEN WE ENTER the dining room, I see Sarah sitting with Peter. As usual she's talking while he's eating and nodding. There's no sign of Hilda, Jane or Richard. I wonder if they've already had lunch. The professor and I take our seats, and as we do, Jane and Richard walk into the dining room — but Hilda isn't with them.

Sarah spots Jane and Richard, too. A strange smile curls up on her face. She's glad that Hilda isn't with them! I can't believe it! Hilda and Sarah have become enemies. Oh no! Living with them in that small cabin will be like being in the middle of a war.

If only I could change cabins. But I know I can't.

I'm stuck with them for the rest of the trip. At least during the day I'll be with the professor in the morning, and I can read in the lounge in the afternoon. But at night it's just me, Hilda and Sarah. What will they do? Shout? Toss hairpins and combs? The look on Hilda's face this morning was as sharp as the knife beside her plate full of toast.

There's nothing I can do about it. I take a deep breath and ask the professor about his talk.

"I'm going to tell the audience about my Iceland expedition," he says. "I'll tell them how I first saw Foula. How it was love at first sight."

The more the professor talks about Foula, the more I want to go there. It's far away from everything — all the terrifying talk of war and torpedoes, Hilda and Sarah snapping at each other like turtles, my grandparents in Worcester who I don't really know and my school in England where I will be the new girl. I wouldn't have to think about any of that on Foula. I could just be there. Safe in a beautiful place.

We finish our dessert — vanilla ice cream with stewed peaches and raisins on top — and I check the dining room to see if Hilda's arrived, but there's no sign of her. Where can she be? What's happened to her?

After lunch the professor goes off to work on his speech. Sarah is parading around the deck with Peter, her arm hooked tightly in his. She nods and smiles at everyone they pass. Peter doesn't smile. He looks like he's been caught in a net and can't find his way out.

I hurry to our cabin to grab my book. I open the door, and there's Hilda lying on her berth in all her clothes, staring at the ceiling. Her eyes are red and puffy. Pins have fallen out of her bun, and strands of her hair stick out every whichaway. Something is wrong when Hilda's hair is a mess.

"Hello, Avis," she mutters. "I … I … I have a crushing headache."

"Can I bring you something to eat? Some broth?" I offer.

"That's kind of you but all I want is … quiet and rest." Hilda's voice cracks. Her eyes shimmer with tears. She brushes them away with the back of her hand.

I've never seen Hilda like this.

"Don't tell Sarah about this. Promise?" she asks me.

"I promise."

"I imagine she's with Peter."

I don't know what to say, but I don't want to lie to Hilda. "Yes. They left the dining room together."

"Did you see … anyone else we know?" she asks.

She means Jane and Richard.

"I had lunch with the professor. I saw Jane and Richard there, too."

"Oh," she says. She swallows hard. "I'm glad the professor has become your friend, Avis. Friendships are important."

I nod. "Can I bring you some tea, a biscuit, an apple? I'm going to the lounge to read and I can stop and get you something."

"Thank you, Avis. You have a kind heart."

Hilda smiles at me. It's a real smile. A warm smile. It's the first time she's ever smiled at me like that. I smile back. I want to ask her what's happened between her, Richard and Jane. I want to know why Sarah is gloating. I want to ask, but I can't.

I turn to go.

"I hope you feel better, Hilda," I say.

Hilda bites her lip. She starts to speak. "I ... I ..." She coughs and clears her throat. "I just need a little time, Avis. That's all."

As I close the cabin door, Hilda turns to the wall. I know she's waiting for me to leave to cry.

Evening • Waiting for the Screams

SARAH AND PETER are eating supper at one end of the dining room. I'm at the other end with the professor and two ladies who are bombarding him with questions about his talk tomorrow night.

"Hello, Avis."

I look up. It's Hilda. Her hair is perfect again. Not a pin is out of place. She sits down beside me, and an elderly couple across the table, the Blooms, introduce themselves. They own a small hat shop in London and were visiting Mrs. Bloom's sister in New York.

They are soon talking about museums and statues in London. Hilda's eyes are fixed on the Blooms the whole time. She doesn't look for Sarah. But Sarah glances at Hilda and scowls.

Oh no! The Hilda and Sarah war rages on! What will it be like when we return to the cabin? Will they want me to take sides? If only I could sleep somewhere else tonight. Even a lifeboat would be nicer than our cabin — unless, of course, some lovebirds sneak in to smooch.

After dinner Hilda and I leave the dining room together. There's a concert in second class, but Hilda doesn't want to go. I'm sure she thinks Richard and Jane might be there, and she doesn't want to see them.

It's a beautiful night and neither of us is in a hurry to get back to our cabin, so we stop to look at the sky. The stars are glowing, the moon is bright, and the sea is as smooth as the lake near my house on a warm spring evening. Passengers stroll around the deck commenting on the sparkling ocean and the starlit sky. Everyone looks happy — as if they don't have a care in the world.

Everyone, except Hilda. Her face has suddenly turned tight and drawn. She looks like she's about to have her tooth extracted. I'm sure she dreads seeing Sarah in our cabin.

But when we arrive back, Sarah's not there. Hilda and I don't say anything, but we're both relieved. We slip into our nightgowns and read in our berths. For an hour it's quiet. Then we hear a clicking and jangling down the hall. The cabin door bursts opens and Sarah sashays in.

"Good evening, ladies," she says in a cheery voice.

Hilda doesn't look up from her book. "Good evening," she says. Her voice is as icy as a winter storm.

I wait for the screams and insults, but the only sound is a clink as Sarah drops her heavy brass bracelet into a wooden box. Then she kicks off her shoes, slides into bed, turns her back to us and is soon fast asleep. Snoring.

Day Five
Wednesday, May 5, 1915

Morning • Hilda Won't Hide

WHEN I WAKE UP, Hilda is not in the cabin. Sarah is sitting at the dressing table combing her hair.

"Oh, you're up," says Sarah. "Hilda dashed out of here early this morning without a word. I know she wants to have breakfast before Jane and Richard arrive. It must have been dreadful to learn that Richard is engaged to a young woman in London. Jane informed her yesterday in a most abrupt manner. I heard about it from Lilah Jones, my new acquaintance. Poor, poor Hilda."

Sarah shakes her head as if Hilda just fell down the stairs and broke both her arms and legs. "Poor Hilda," she says again, but she doesn't sound sorry at all.

"Hilda was talking to a nice couple at dinner last night," I tell her as I slip on my dress.

"I noticed." Sarah purses her lips. "They're quite old, aren't they? Poor Hilda. It's terrible to be interested in someone and discover they're not the least bit interested in you. I'd want to hide in my cabin for the rest of the trip."

"Well, Hilda isn't hiding so that's good." I can't believe that I'm defending Hilda, but I hate Sarah's sarcastic tone.

"Well, listen to you, Avis Dolphin, sticking up for Hilda. What has come over you on this trip?"

"Nothing," I say. "It's just that sometimes, Sarah, you sound … mean."

Sarah gasps. Her mouth hangs open. "Mean? How could you say something so cruel and untrue, Avis?"

I want to shout at her, "It's true and you know it!" But I don't.

"I have to go, Sarah." I shut the cabin door, relieved to be out of there. I race down the hall to the dining room.

Hilda is sitting beside the Blooms. She's smiling, talking, listening. She looks up and waves at me to come over. She smiles as warmly as yesterday.

The Blooms ask me about my trip, my family, my plans in England. They tell me that I must visit them in London and meet their niece's daughter, who's my age. They tell Hilda they'll introduce her to their daughter and son-in-law who know "lovely, eligible young men." Hilda is trying not to look too excited, but she's smiling so widely that it's clear she is. It's time for me to meet the professor, so I scoop up my last bit of egg.

"Please tell the professor we are eager to hear him speak tonight," says Hilda.

"I will. See you later."

As I leave the dining room, I glance back. Hilda and the Blooms are still talking. Hilda looks comfortable, happy, hopeful — not like a "poor Hilda" at all.

The professor is waiting for me beside my deck chair. His eyes are sparkling. "Avis!" he exclaims. "I just saw a porpoise leap. It was magical! I wish you were here. They rarely come to the surface."

"Wow! I wish I'd seen it, too."

"Let's watch the sea. Maybe we'll be lucky. Maybe it will return."

We peer over the railing. We look for bubbles, movement, anything to tell us that a porpoise is about to leap up. We stare at the ocean for a half hour — but nothing.

"Shall we walk on?" The professor turns away.

"Just one more minute," I say, and as I do, a small bubble appears on the surface of the ocean. "Professor, look!" My heart pounds so loudly I can hear it in my ears.

The professor and I stare at the sea. I hold my breath as the bubble grows bigger and bigger and then, like something out of a dream, a dark gray creature with a flat snout, a long body and a sharp triangular fin leaps out of the sea.

"It's a porpoise!" exclaims the professor.

The porpoise leaps up once more and then dives down quickly. I stare at the bubbles it leaves behind till they fade away.

"I can't believe I saw a porpoise leaping out of the ocean!" I say.

"It's a gift from the sea," says the professor.

We gaze at the ocean for another half hour hoping the porpoise will return, but it doesn't.

"If I saw a mermaid, I'd be so thrilled my heart would stop," I say. "Ever since you told me about the mermaid near Foula, I've dreamed about mermaids. Imagine if they were real."

"Who knows? Maybe they are. The old timers on Foula swear they've seen mermaids. The ocean is full of strange creatures. There's a vast, hidden, beautiful world beneath the sea, where no man has traveled. Not yet, at least."

"Except in stories, of course! Your stories take me to enchanted places and to times long ago. So please tell me more about Jill. How does she escape from the bogeyman and the giant? Will the mermaid help her again?"

"Jill is terrified but she keeps her wits about her."

I close my eyes and picture Jill, determined never to give up. The professor makes her so real, I feel like she's my friend. I wish she were my friend.

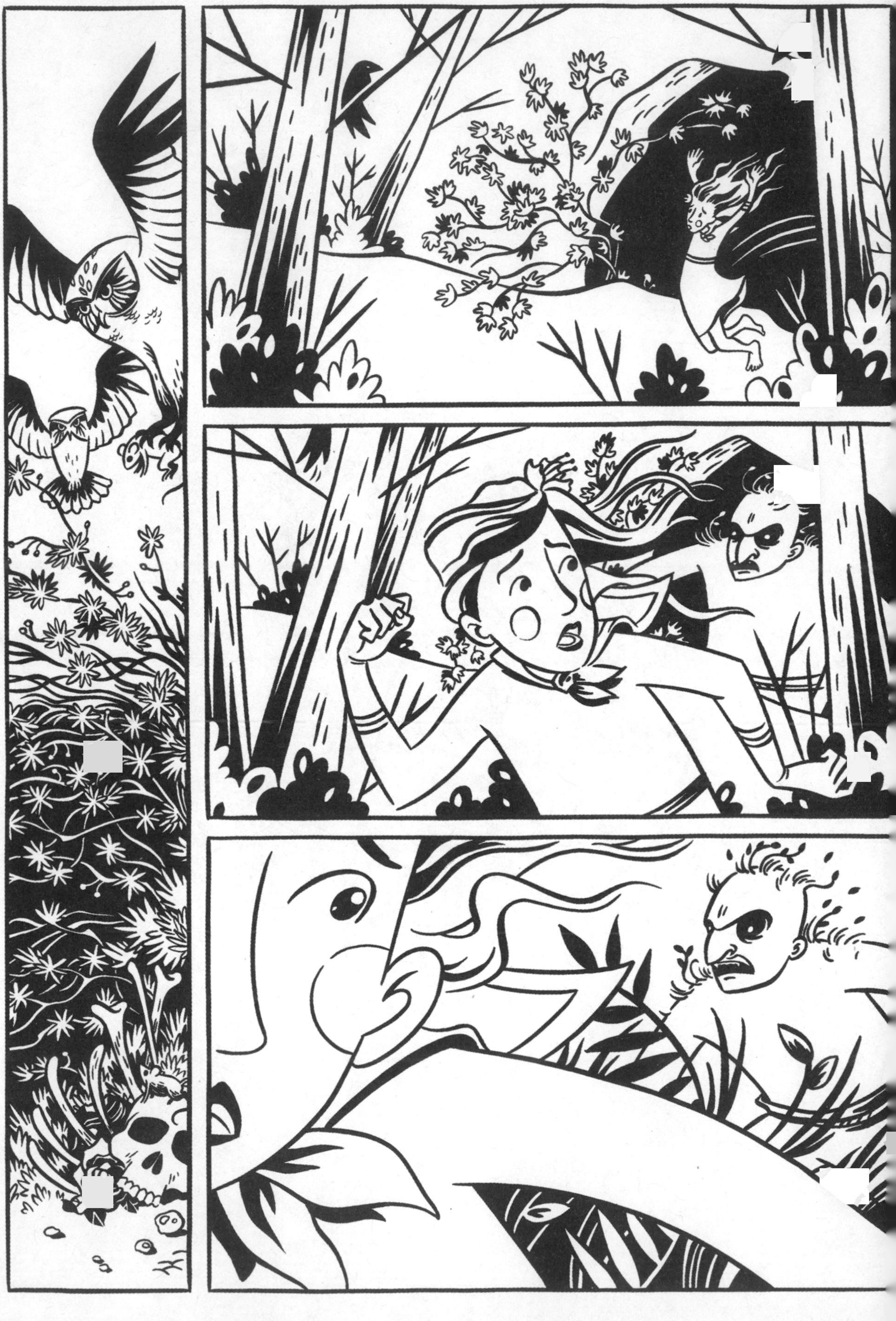

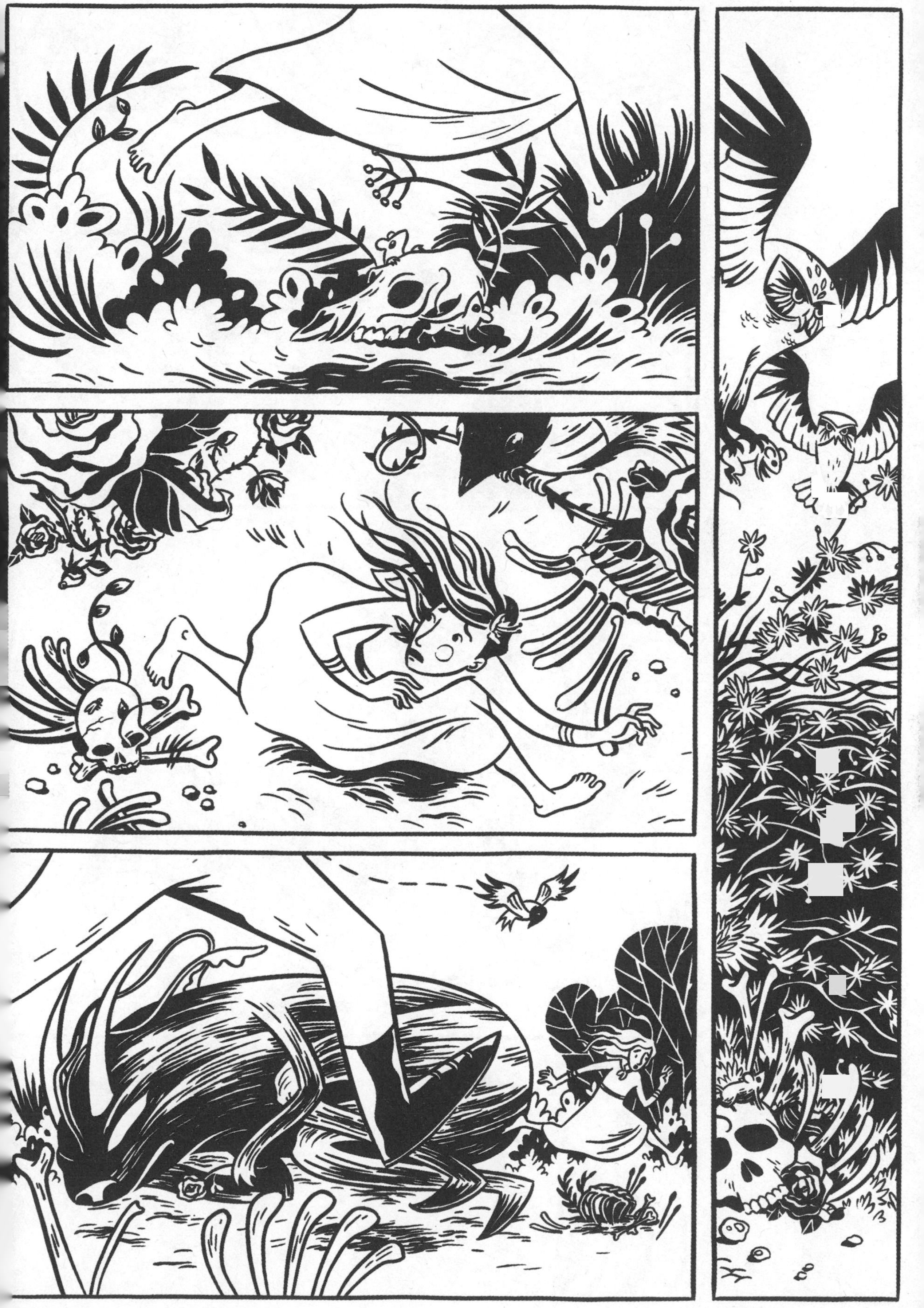

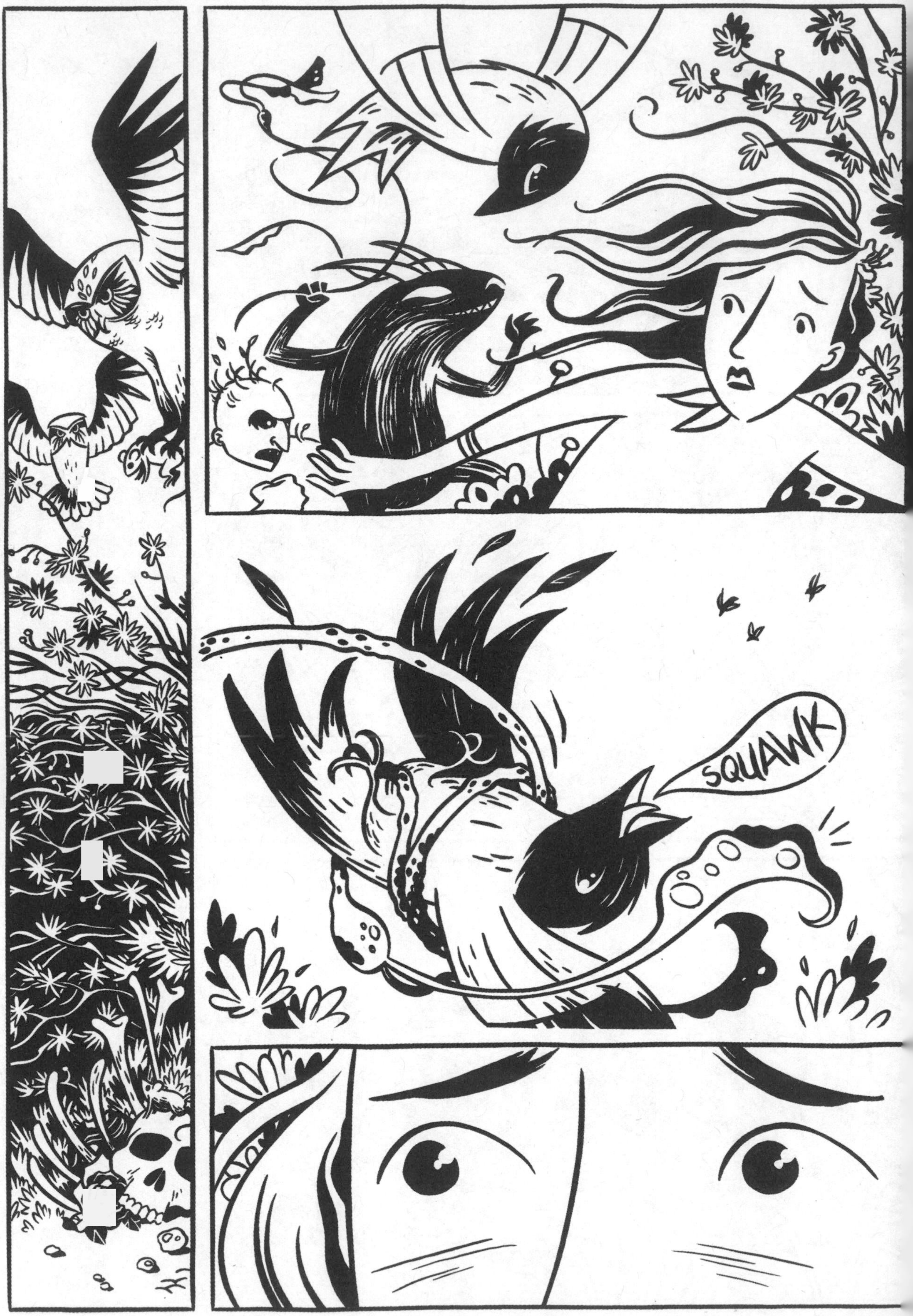
SQUAWK

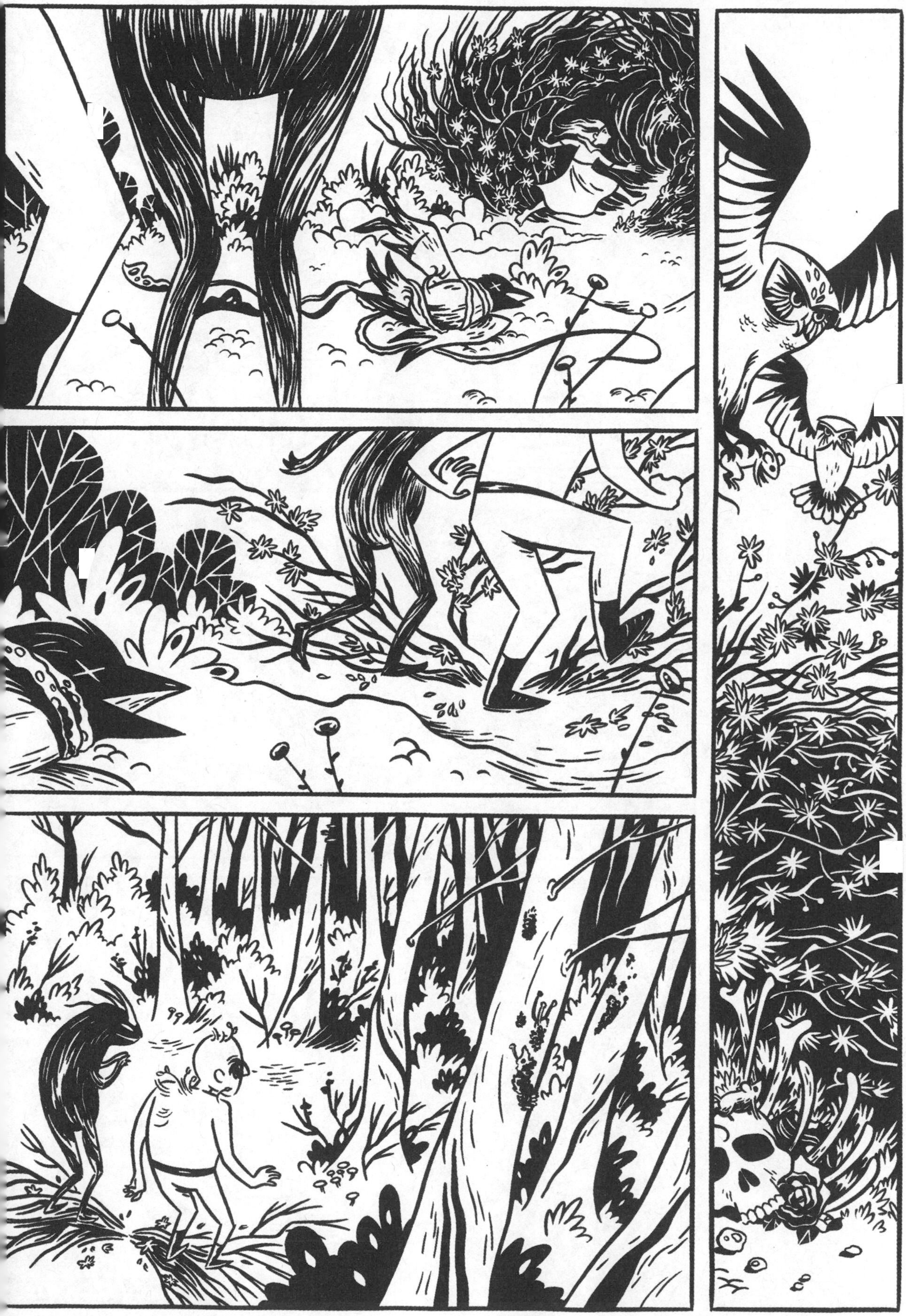

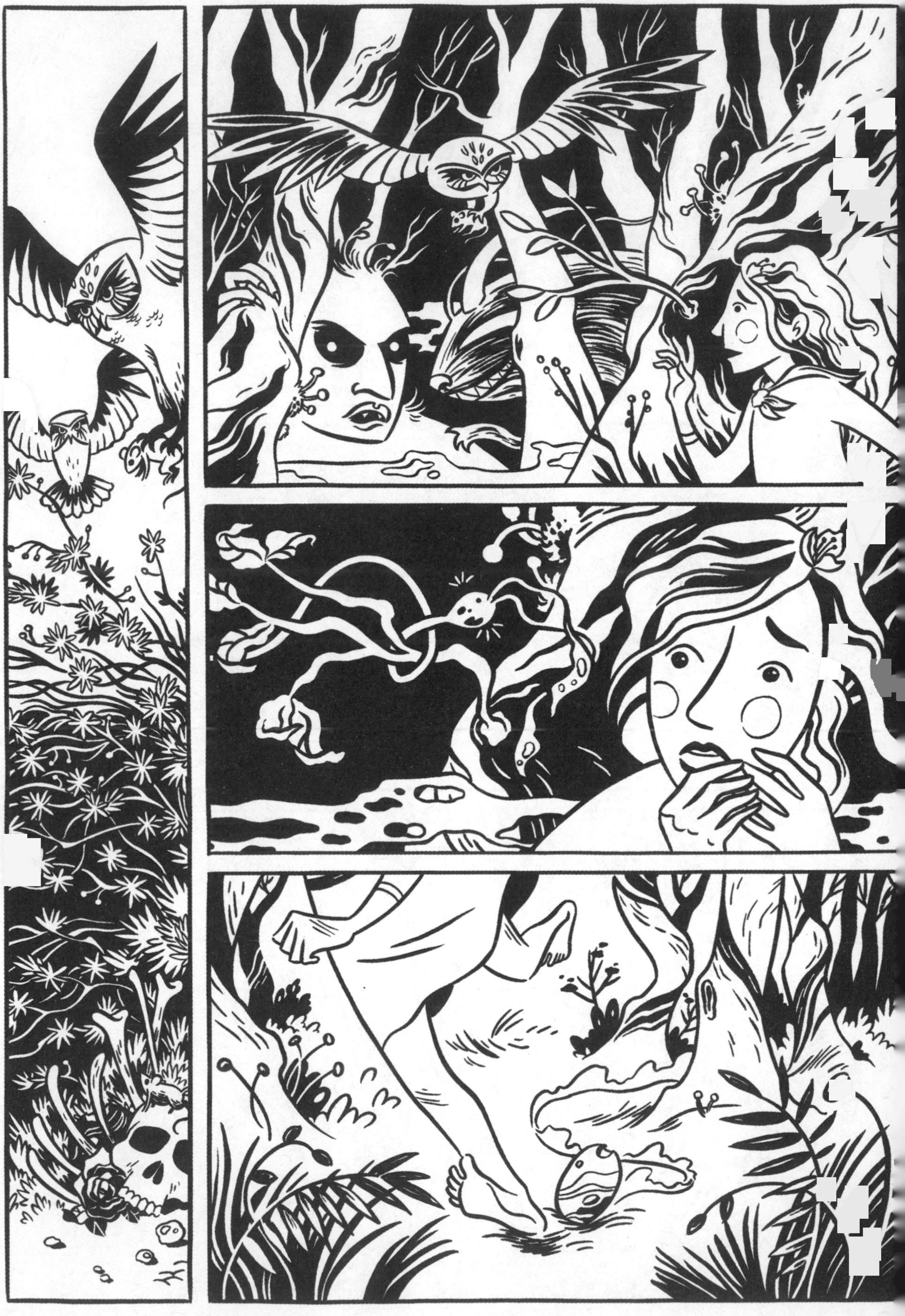

"Jill runs as fast as she can," says the professor. "She is … ouch!"

A medicine ball grazes the professor's leg. Two boys were tossing the ball near us.

"Sorry, sir," says one of the boys. He's tall and lanky. He brushes his black hair out of his eyes. "Are you OK, sir?"

"I'm fine," says the professor, pitching the heavy ball back to him.

The boys mutter sorry again and hurry away.

"It's not just German U-boats we have to worry about," I say. "Those medicine balls are weapons."

The professor laughs. "You're right. Look! This deck is as busy as a schoolyard."

I was so absorbed in Jill's story that I hadn't noticed anything else. The deck is bursting with activity. Children jump rope. Some play tag. Others race with spoons, potatoes and hard-boiled eggs.

"I won! I won!" shouts a young girl with curly brown hair after a round of the egg-and-spoon race. She jumps up and down. She beams when she's presented with a ribbon for her victory.

Then she turns and bounds over to us. "Remember me? I met you the first day, right before we sailed. You're a dolphin!"

I laugh. "I remember you and you're right. My name is Avis Dolphin. You said that I belong at sea because of my name. What's your name?"

"I am Ailsa Booth-Jones," she says. "And look

what I've won!" She holds out three gold ribbons and a tiny gold-covered brooch shaped like a ship. She points to the brooch. "This is my favorite. I won first prize in the spelling game. I'm going to keep this ship forever."

"It's pretty," I say.

"Can you pin it on my sweater, please?" Ailsa asks.

I pin her brooch on her pale blue sweater.

"How does it look?" Ailsa parades around us like a model.

"Beautiful. It will remind you of the fun you had on the *Lusy*."

"Isn't the *Lusy* the best ship in the world? I wish the trip would go on forever. Well, goodbye now." Ailsa waves and skips off to join her friends.

I think of the small wooden ship my father carved for me. I'll always keep it. No matter what.

The professor and I walk along the deck. We pause to watch a group of six adults playing shuffleboard. Each player pushes the metal disk toward the right spot on the chalked space. The players are as keen as Ailsa to win and just as disappointed when they don't.

"Missed it by an inch!" says a man, slapping his thigh.

"Mine's in!" says a woman, pirouetting in place.

I know her and the man beside her! They're the smoochers from the lifeboat. I don't think they recognize us. They were too busy scooting away to notice anyone yesterday.

The professor and I walk on till two couples approach us.

"What do you know about the German spies they caught yesterday, Professor?" asks a slim woman wearing a dark blue skirt and matching jacket. "My husband and I just heard about it at breakfast and we're worried."

"Were they planning to blow up the ship or take hostages?" asks her husband. "I read the papers. I know what the Germans can do. They don't care if there are innocent women and children aboard."

"No one knows if they are spies or just stowaways," the professor reassures them. "But I understand that the men will be interrogated on shore. Meanwhile they're in cabins below the waterline."

"Well, that's good news. Glad we caught those Germans in time," says the man.

He tucks his wife's arm into his and they stroll off.

The professor shakes his head. "Those poor stowaways don't stand a chance if there's an emergency. They'll never reach a lifeboat in time. Remember, Avis, if anything happens, you must find me."

"I will."

I'm glad the professor is looking out for me, but if something terrible were to happen how would I find him? How would he find me? What if he didn't? What would I do? What could anyone do?

"Come on," says the professor. "Let's have lunch and forget about stowaways and disasters at sea. I hope there's ice cream for dessert."

"Me, too."

I shake my head, trying to banish my worry. Think about ice cream instead, I tell myself. Rich, creamy, melt-in-your-mouth chocolate ice cream.

Afternoon • Promises

We reach the dining room. Sarah is at one end of a long table. She's sitting with Peter, as usual. Hilda is at the other end with that nice elderly couple, the Blooms. Jane and Richard are far away from Hilda at another table. I'm sure Hilda is glad about that.

I check the menu. "There's ice cream!" I tell the professor.

He beams. "Strawberry for me!" He sounds as excited as Ailsa when she won the egg-and-spoon race.

After a lunch of thick beef stew, we both have a bowl of ice cream. Mine is chocolate, of course. The ice cream is so luscious we lick our spoons and don't leave a drop in the bowl.

"I'm tempted to ask for seconds," the professor whispers, "but I'd better review my notes and practice my jokes for tonight's talk."

"Hilda, Sarah and I will be there to cheer you on."

"Can I count on you, Avis, to laugh at my jokes even if they aren't funny?" he says.

"I promise to laugh. And I will make sure that Hilda and Sarah laugh, too. If they don't I'll poke them."

"They aren't sitting together lately, are they?"

"They're barely speaking to each other. They used to be friends but it's war in our cabin now," I say. "Luckily we're only together a few more days. And luckily I have you for a friend, Professor."

The professor smiles. "I'm glad we're friends, Avis. Spending time with you is like being with my boys. And it's a delight sharing Foula with you."

"I love Foula already. I can't wait to see it."

"And you will. One day soon, I promise. Now I'm off to rehearse those jokes. I don't want anyone to throw eggs or tomatoes tonight. That would be a real disaster at sea!"

The professor leaves and I suddenly feel sad. I don't know why. Maybe it's because we're nearing shore. Maybe it's because there's so much that will be new for me in England. Maybe it's because in less than two days I'll have to say goodbye to the professor. He feels like family. The best kind of family.

Evening • Bravo and Jokes

IT'S NINE O'CLOCK, and Hilda, the Blooms and I sit in the second row of the second-class lounge and wait for the professor's talk to begin.

It's my first night out on the ship, and I'm so excited that I can't stop smiling. Hilda is smiling, too. She's promised to laugh at the professor's jokes. I made Sarah promise, too, and she said she'd make sure Peter laughed as well. That makes six people laughing already!

The room fills up quickly. People whisper that Mr. Vanderbilt may show up for the talk. He's interested in exploration and has heard about the professor's adventures in Iceland.

"Look who's just come in!" says a short, stocky man behind me. "Rich man Vanderbilt. All the way from first class."

I turn around to look. Mr. Vanderbilt is dressed in an elegant dark suit with a pink carnation stuck in his buttonhole. He nods to the people gawking at him and sits down in a back row.

"You know Vanderbilt's friends serve foie gras, that expensive pâté, to their dogs. And those dogs are served by footmen in fancy uniforms," says the stocky man. "It's a great life if you're a rich man's dog."

"But I hear Vanderbilt is a good fellow. Not arrogant like some of his wealthy friends," says his companion. "And look at him coming to second class to hear a talk."

In a few minutes the room is packed. There's no space left to sit, so a row of people stand at the back. The professor's talk is about to begin. My heart pounds as if my best friend or my father were going to speak. I want everyone to love the professor's talk. I want everyone to laugh at his jokes.

The professor walks in and heads for the front

row. He sees me and winks his right eye. I wink back with my left. The professor stretches out his legs and leans back in his chair.

A tall man in a dark suit approaches the front of the lounge. He introduces the professor as a distinguished teacher, a speaker, a writer, an intrepid explorer and the Laird of Foula, a tiny island in Scotland.

The professor stands up and begins. His voice is strong, clear, confident. There's not a sound in the room. Everyone's eyes are on him as he tells us how he and his friend Mr. Barrett sailed to Iceland on an expedition headed by Mr. F. W. W. Howell. They were the first to cross a vast ridge of magnificent ice fields. Mr. Howell kept records and the professor kept a diary, but when Mr. Howell died, the only record of the expedition that survived was the professor's.

He reads from his diary. He sprinkles jokes throughout his talk, and no one needs poking. Everyone laughs! He explains how he spotted Foula for the first time on his way to Iceland. By the time the expedition was over he was determined to buy it.

"Friends and family thought I was out of my mind to buy such a remote and wild island, but Foula's magic drew me. It still does. Thank you for listening to my talk and may we all have a safe journey."

The room bursts into applause. I can't stop smiling again. I am so proud of the professor.

"Any questions?" he asks.

A man standing at the back calls out. It's that

woman Wanda's husband. The man who barked at her not to worry when they watched the lifeboat drill yesterday.

"I have a question, sir. Why do you terrify people by questioning the procedures our captain has put in place for our safety? The captain is in charge of this ship. Do you know more than the captain? Have you ever been in charge of a huge ocean liner like the *Lusitania*?"

Everyone is stunned by the man's mocking tone and his angry comments, which have nothing to do with the professor's talk.

But the professor looks calmly at the man. He answers in a steady, even voice.

"I have never been the captain of a ship like the *Lusitania*," he says, "but I'm an experienced sailor. I believe we should all ask questions, especially when there are lives at stake. I respect the captain, but I hope the captain and others who disagree with me are willing to listen to suggestions with an open mind."

"Bravo! Well said, Professor Holbourn."

Everyone turns to see who is defending the professor. It's Mr. Vanderbilt!

"Let's give our esteemed speaker, Professor Holborn, another round of applause," he says, standing up. "Let's tell him how much we appreciate his talk and his thoughtful suggestions for our safety."

Everyone stands up and we applaud again, loudly and long. I want to hug Mr. Vanderbilt!

When the applause dies down, people mob the professor, shake his hand, pat him on the back, tell him that his talk was inspiring and promise to read his work. I wave to the professor but so many people surround him, he doesn't see me. Hilda and I head back to our cabin.

"What a fantastic talk. What a spirit of adventure! And what dignity the professor showed with that heckler," she says.

I nod.

"And wasn't that kind of Mr. Vanderbilt to stand up for him?" says Hilda.

"It was," I say. "I could have kissed Mr. Vanderbilt for that."

"Avis Dolphin!" says Hilda in a shocked voice. But then she smiles the new Hilda smile.

I like this new Hilda — much more than the old one. I'm glad she's met the Blooms. And if she meets an eligible young man in London, I know that she will be an even happier Hilda.

We reach our cabin, and Sarah is not there. She's still away when I climb into my berth. I pick up Father's small ship and hold it. I close my eyes and imagine walking beside Jill on a rocky Foula beach. I can almost hear the wind whistle and whoosh. It feels so close that I open my eyes.

It's not the wind whooshing.

It's Hilda.

Snoring.

Day Six
Thursday, May 6, 1915

Morning • Clanging and Banging

I WAKE UP TO banging. I peek through the porthole. There's just a sliver of sun. Why is there so much noise so early? What's going on?

I toss off my covers and peer down. Sarah and Hilda are sound asleep. They are both snoring, but Hilda is snoring louder. She sounds like a barking dog. Sarah's snore is softer, but her mouth hangs open like a fish.

I slide off the top berth and down to the floor. The bed squeaks and Sarah mumbles, "Please don't. Don't!" Is she dreaming about Peter? I imagine the two of them snuggling in the lifeboat, and I bite my lip so I won't laugh. I dress quickly and scribble a note:

I'm out on deck to see the sun rise.
See you at breakfast,
Avis

I pull the cabin door closed and race down the hall to the deck. There's more banging. Then a clunk and a clatter. Oh no! My stomach knots. Has the ship been hit? Has it slammed into something? We're not near any icebergs, so it can't be that.

A crewman dashes out.

"What's going on?" I ask him. "Has something happened to the ship?"

"Nothing's happened, miss. Nothing to worry about. Just a precaution. The captain ordered the lifeboats swung over the sides of the ship so we can lower them quickly if that were ever needed."

The crewman hurries away. His reassurances don't make me feel better. My stomach still feels like someone twisted it.

I look out and watch the sun rise. It lights up the deck, the chairs, the ship and my face. The ocean glows red, yellow and orange, like a painting that keeps changing.

The banging stops, and the knot in my stomach loosens. I breathe in the cool morning air. There's a whiff of salt, but it's not strong or unpleasant. I have my sea legs now! It's strange and wonderful to be on deck alone. I feel like I have the *Lusy*, the sky and the sea all to myself.

Below and above, people are sleeping. Farther below, men are stoking the coals and tossing them into the flames to keep the ship moving. In the galley kitchen, staff cut, stir, bake, and arrange trays that will soon sail out into a bustling dining room for breakfast. But nobody is going to breakfast yet.

I stretch out my arms, close my eyes and take deep, long breaths.

When I open my eyes, I'm not alone. A couple stands beside me. The woman rubs her eyes. She looks like she just crawled out of bed. Her hair has been pulled back into a crooked bun. Some of the man's shirt buttons are open, and the thick hair on his chest peeks out.

"What was all that racket about?" the man asks me.

I repeat what the crewman said.

"Do you believe that? We're in trouble, I tell you. Big trouble."

His wife pokes him in the arm. "Harold, you're scaring this young lady. Isn't it enough that you frighten me every day with your rants about German U-boats? Leave her alone."

"I'm not scaring you, am I, miss?" asks Harold.

I shrug. "You're not the only one who's worried," I tell him. "But we'll be fine. At least, I hope so."

"We're not going to be torpedoed, Harold," says his wife. "Didn't the captain reassure you of that when you plied him with your endless questions after the professor's talk? Come on. Let's go inside for breakfast." She tugs at his sleeve.

"I'll be there in a minute, Mildred. I want to breathe some more of this good, clean sea air."

I wish Harold would follow his wife to the dining room. I don't want to hear what he's going to say. But Harold just inches closer.

"So what does your friend the professor think about our chances of making it to shore in one piece?" he asks me. "I see you two walking around the deck all the time."

"The professor thinks the *Lusitania* is strong and solid but he wishes there were lifeboat drills for the passengers."

"He's right. By the way, my name is Harold Mosley." He thrusts out his hand, and I shake it.

"I'm Avis Dolphin."

"Avis Dolphin! What a perfect name for the ocean! As for me, I hate the ocean. Always have. Can't swim and don't want to. After all, who knows what creatures will grab you under there." Harold points down to the water and shudders. "Sharks, eels, giant squids? The ocean is full of them. I wish I hadn't said yes to this trip. But Mildred insisted. She wants to visit her family in London. Her nephew is off to fight in a few weeks. I knew it was risky. I read the German warning in the papers. All I can say is keep your eyes open and jump off this ship at the first sign of trouble, Avis Dolphin. Can you swim?"

"Yes, but I've never gone swimming in the ocean. There are lifebelts for everyone on the ship."

"Big, clumsy things, aren't they? Hard to put on. And I won't put one on no matter what happens. I'm terrified of water. Oh, it's fine from up here. Pretty, actually. But don't drop me into that icy ocean. I'd die of fright as soon as my feet touched the water." Harold looks out to sea and sighs. Then he turns and shakes my hand again, "Good luck to you, Avis Dolphin. Good luck to us all. We'll need it."

Harold heads toward the dining room. Why did he have to tell me his fears? My stomach is in knots again. But he's not the only person who is worried today. We're closer to shore, and the deck is packed with people now. Some are as nervous as Harold.

"Will the British Admiralty escort us safely to shore?" asks a tall, thin-as-a-rail woman near me.

"Of course! They have to protect us. It's their duty," says her short, curly-haired friend.

"I heard telegrams arrived yesterday for the captain. U-boats are hovering near shore. We're in danger," says a woman in a long black cape.

"Stop fretting, Dora! We'll outrun those U-boats," says her husband. "You always imagine the worst."

I walk toward the dining room, glad to escape the talk of war and torpedoes.

"Oh, there you are, Avis," says Sarah, waving to me to come over. "Did you see the sun rise?"

"Yes."

Sarah turns and jabbers on to Peter about what they should visit in London. I can't believe it! Sarah is planning their future! She's also ordered a huge breakfast of fried eggs, toast, jam and pancakes and is nibbling as she talks. Peter has ordered the exact same breakfast, but he's too busy gulping it down to say anything. Then again, maybe he doesn't want to say anything. Maybe he likes just nodding and eating.

Neither of them is concerned about nearing the shore. They're not worried about U-boats. They're not anxious about anything except the coffee.

"It's too bitter," says Sarah. "I must call the waiter."

"Yes," says Peter, his mouth full of banana pancake.

Peter and Sarah sound like an old, married couple! Not only are they eating the same food, they're complaining about the same food!

I walk over to Hilda at the other end of the table. She's talking to the Blooms. They invite me to sit down beside them. They're worried that shopping in London has been affected by the war and there will be less good-quality clothing to buy.

"Oh no!" says Hilda. "I was looking forward to buying a new dress and a new hat."

"Don't worry, dear," says Mrs. Bloom, patting her arm. "We'll make sure you find the perfect hat. As for a dress, I'm sure the shortages are only temporary. The war will be over in no time."

"Maybe it will even end before our big family event," says Mr. Bloom. "Our daughter's husband joins his army unit in a few weeks. He swears he'll be back by summer, in time for the birth of our first grandchild."

The Blooms beam. They can't wait to be grand-parents. The Blooms and Hilda aren't worried about U-boats, either.

I order a fried egg and a pancake, but my stomach still aches. Harold's words echo in my head. *We're in trouble. Big trouble.* I push the food around on my plate and nibble at it, but nothing tastes good. Not even the maple syrup on the pancake.

"I have to go. I'm meeting the professor," I finally say.

"You've hardly touched your food, dear," says Mrs. Bloom.

"I'm not hungry. I'll eat later."

I dash out of the dining room.

The professor leans against our chair, looking out to sea. He has a far-away look in his eyes. I know he can't wait to see his family and Foula. He turns and smiles when he sees me.

"Your jokes were perfect last night," I tell him. "I didn't have to poke anyone. Everyone loved your talk, except that awful man at the back. I wanted to throw a tomato at him."

The professor grins. "I appreciate that, Avis. As for my jokes, I'm glad they went over well. I rehearsed them longer than my whole talk. It's not easy being funny!"

"I loved how Mr. Vanderbilt stood up for you. He's your fan, Professor."

"He was very kind. We spoke after my talk. He's

interested in exploration and he's fascinated by Foula. I invited him to visit us there."

"I wonder if Mr. Vanderbilt heard the banging this morning in first class. A crewman said they were swinging the lifeboats."

"I saw the lifeboats swung over. Rumors are flying all over the ship now that we're nearing shore."

"Our trip is almost over. So please tell me what happens next on Foula. Will Jill be safe? Will she be rescued?"

The professor smiles. "Ah yes! Our Jill will find a way. She's like you, Avis, determined and brave, even when she's scared."

"You think I'm brave?"

"I know you're brave. Look how well you deal with Sarah and Hilda. Look how you handle being away from home. Look how you stood up for me with the captain. As for Jill …"

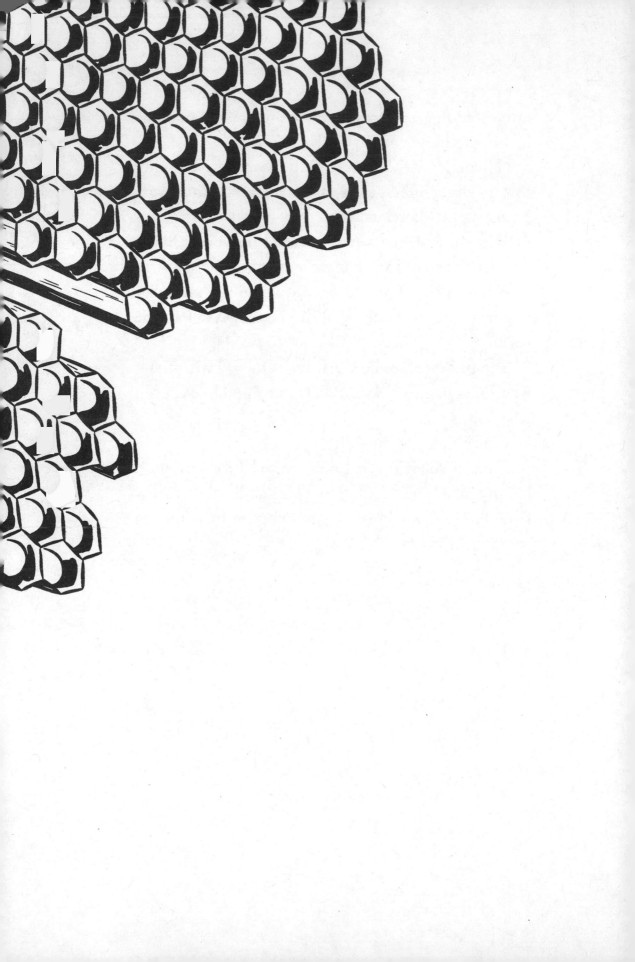

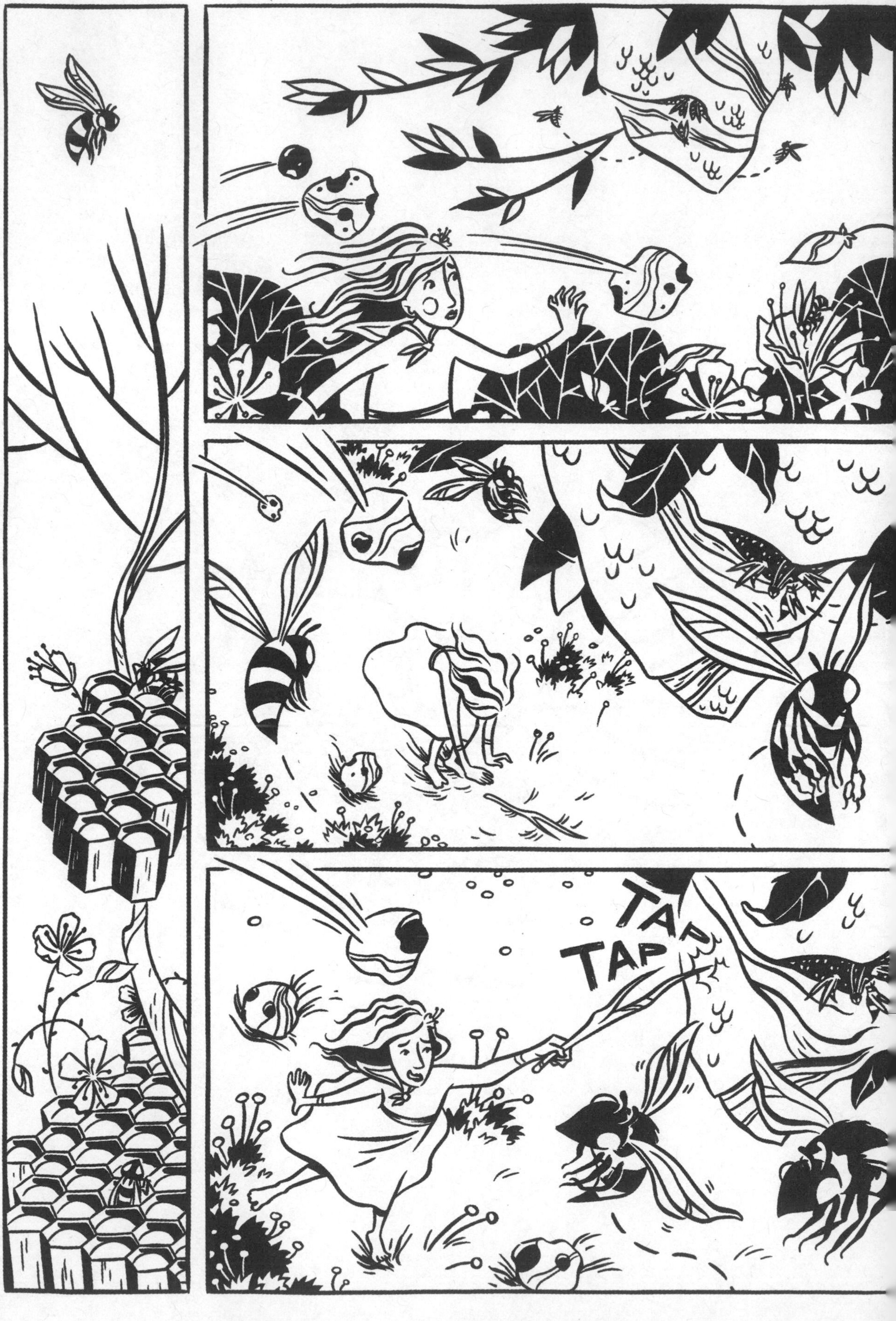
TAP
TAP

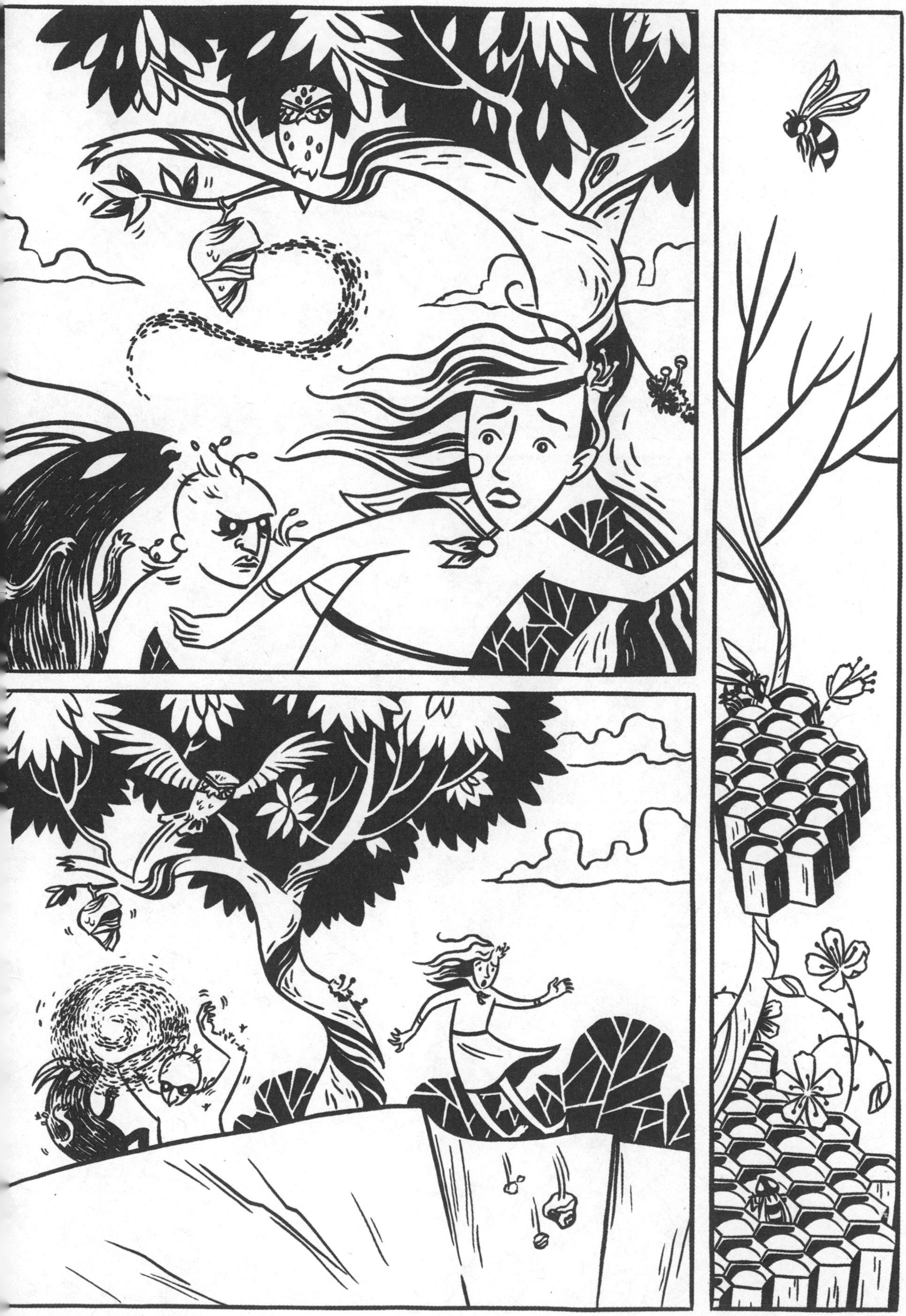

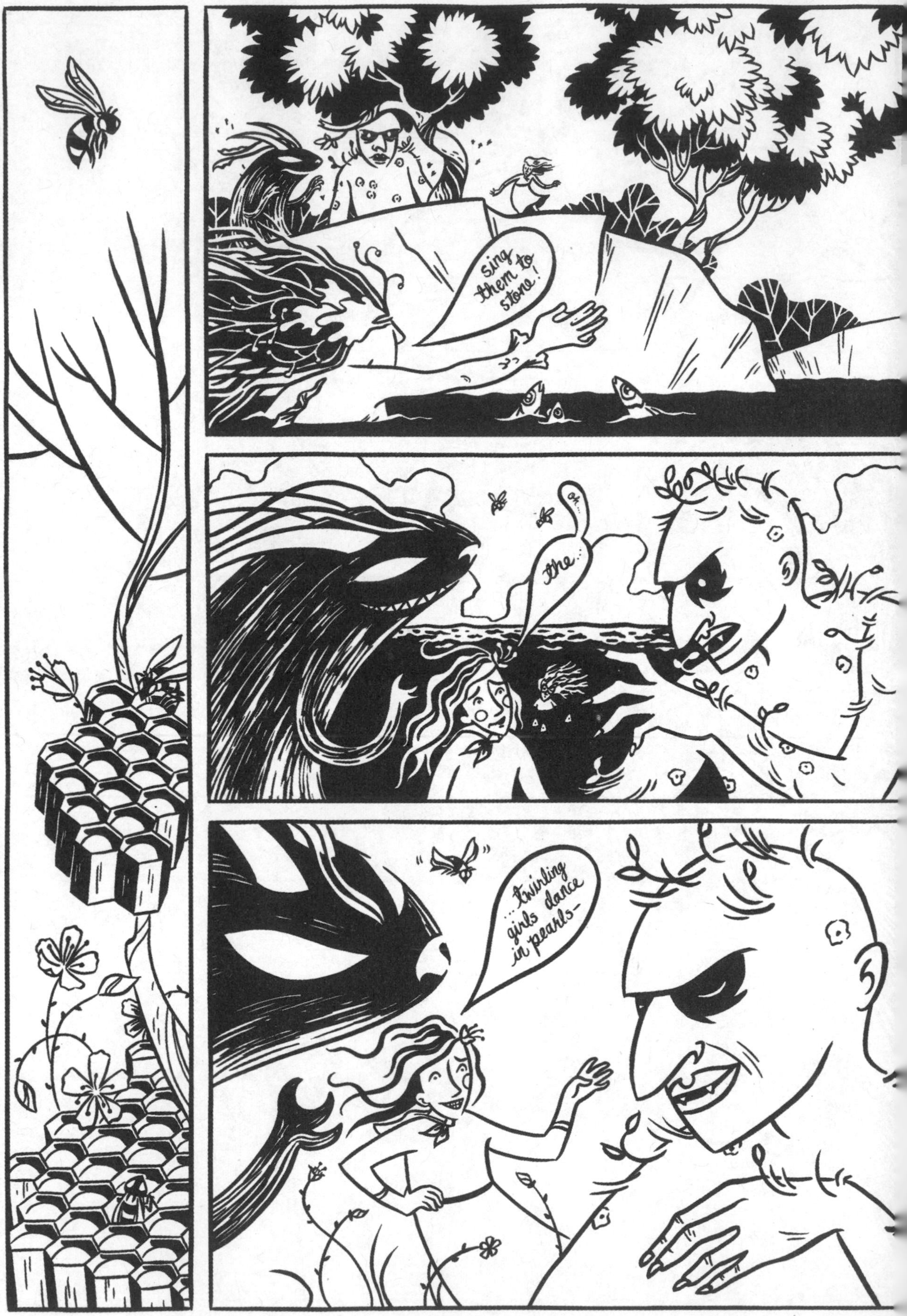
sing them to stone!
oh...
the...
...twirling girls dance in pearls-

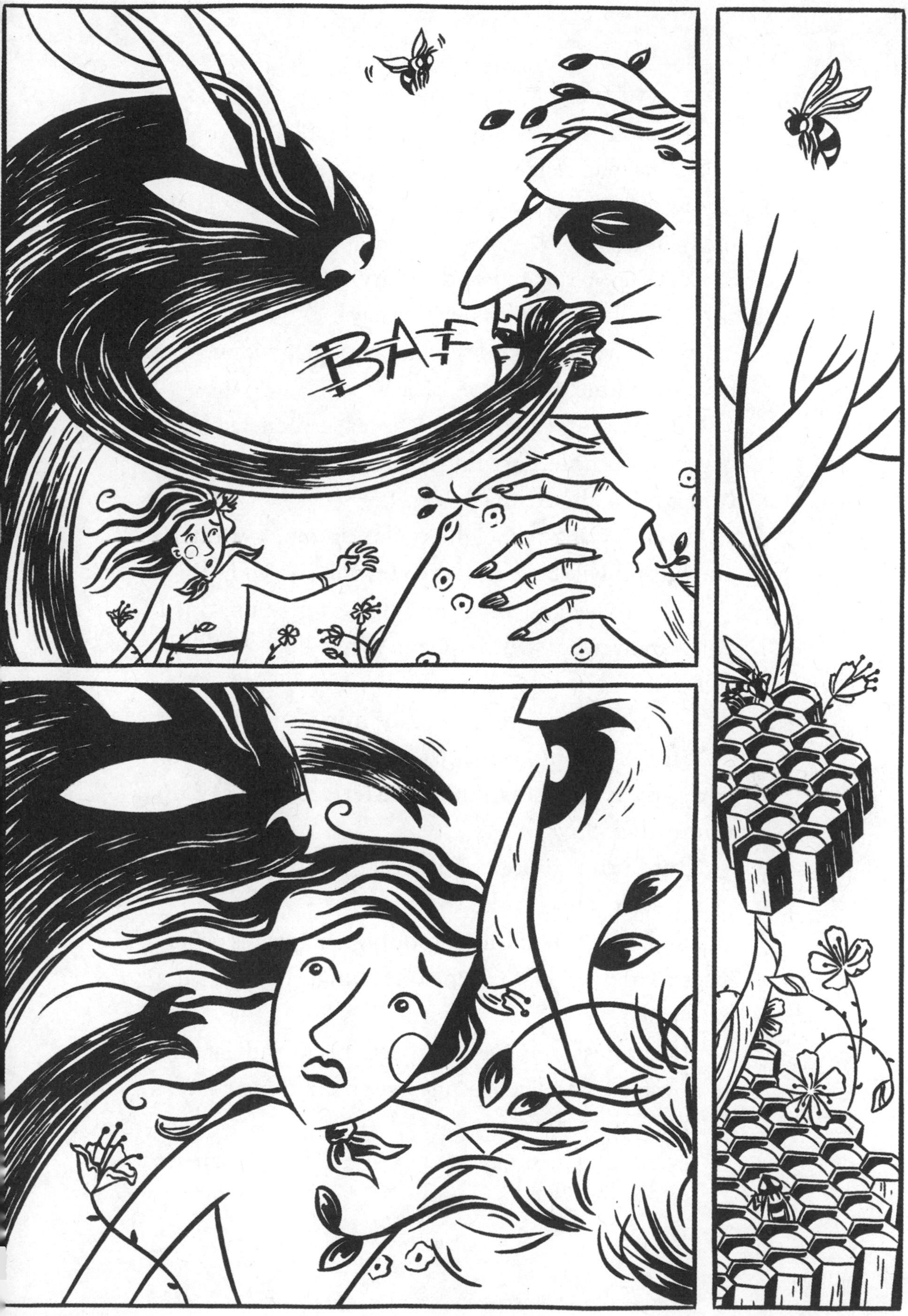
BAF

The professor stops speaking and looks out to sea.

"What happens next?" I ask. His eyes have that far-away look again. It's like he's sailing to Foula already.

"Let's leave the end of the story till tomorrow," he says. "We'll finish it on our last day."

"But I want to know what happens today. You have to tell me, Professor. Please."

"Ah, Avis, storytellers like to leave their listeners begging for more, dangling at a suspenseful moment. It heightens the drama."

"I don't want to heighten the drama. I want to know if Jill will be safe. Do you think she will?"

"Jill is brave and smart and doesn't give up. But I don't know what will happen. What do you think, Avis?"

"It's your story, Professor. Not mine."

"Stories belong to the listener, too. It's your story now, just as much as mine. You're free to make up your own ending."

"But I want to hear your ending, Professor."

He shakes his head. "Tomorrow."

I sigh. Despite all my prodding the professor refuses to budge. "Just tell me one thing," I ask. "Is it a happy ending?"

The professor tosses his head back and laughs. "You want Jill to live happily ever after, don't you?"

"Yes! Don't you?"

"Well, all I can say is that she'll face whatever

comes her way with courage. That's a happy ending already!"

"No, it's not." I roll my eyes. "Professor, you're impossible."

"Maybe, but I'm still saving the end of the story till tomorrow. It will be like dessert at the end of a meal. Then all will be revealed. Meanwhile, why don't we walk to all our favorite places on the *Lusy* and say goodbye. Let's start with the elevator to first class."

We revisit everything — the gilded elevator, the plush first-class dining room, the elegant public rooms and hallways. We admire the chandeliers again and swivel in three fancy chairs.

But something feels different today. People gather in small groups. Their faces are pinched with worry. They wonder if we will be safe. Many have heard the rumors of U-boats. Many believe the rumors. Some plan to try on their lifebelts today. Others are certain it's all ridiculous and unnecessary.

After lunch we stroll around second class. We look at the lifeboats dangling over the side of the ship.

"No one is smooching in there now," I say.

The professor and I laugh at the thought of a couple kissing in a swinging lifeboat. "All that swinging would make me throw up," I say.

A group of passengers holds a meeting near us. They set up a committee to teach everyone, especially the children, how to put on their lifebelts. A man approaches Captain Turner and asks him to approve their idea.

He huffs and puffs, but he finally relents. "It's fine with me if it makes you feel better. Just be sure you're not creating a panic. Panic is the real enemy on a ship. We'll be fine. You have my guarantee."

"Look at the captain's face," I whisper to the professor. "It's as tight as his collar. And his nose is twitching. I think he's worried, too. Even with his guarantee."

"You're right, Avis. But let's forget about all of that for now and have one last adventure on the *Lusy*."

"What kind of adventure?"

"Let's sneak into the first-class talent show tonight. It's a performance to raise money for seamen."

I clap my hands. "Let's do it!"

The professor and I agree to meet after dinner. Then he hurries off to work on a newspaper article about his travels in America.

Late Afternoon • In the Belly of the Ship

I GO BACK TO our cabin. Hilda and Sarah are out. I grab my book and race to the lounge. I sink into one of the big chairs and try to read, but I can't keep my mind on Matt and John's adventures today. All I can think about is that in less than a day and a half we'll be in England. I don't want to say goodbye to the professor. When will I see him again? And what will it be like to meet my grandparents? And how will it feel to attend a new school and meet new classmates?

I wish Lizzie were going to my new school. It wouldn't feel so strange to start school in a new place if Lizzie were there. I promise myself to write to her as soon as we land. She'll want to know every detail about the *Lusy*. She'll ask if I've visited every part of the ship, and I haven't. Not third class. OK, then. Third class, here I come! I tuck my book under my arm, scoot out of the lounge and head down the stairs.

As soon as I'm in third class, everything looks and feels different. There are no elegant tables or plush chairs anywhere. There are no beautiful lights hanging overhead. Everything is plain, bare and blindingly white, and metal pipes stick out from the walls. I don't feel like I'm in a fancy, floating hotel. I feel like I'm in the belly of the ship, especially since the ship rocks more down here.

I peek into the empty dining room. It's spotlessly clean, but there are no white pillars or soft chairs. Just long, polished wooden tables and wooden chairs with metal legs. I walk in further. There's a dark blue cap under a table. I lean over to pick it up.

"Hey!" says a boy. "That's mine!"

A boy my age with dark brown, curly hair is standing behind me. "I just came in to look for that. It's my cap!"

I hand it to him. "I'm Avis Dolphin."

The boy plunks the cap on his head. "I'm Norman McGuire. I've never seen you before. And I've met everyone in third class."

"I'm from second class."

"What are you doing down here?"

"I promised my best friend I'd explore all of the ship and I hadn't seen third class."

"It's not as posh as up there," says Norman, pointing. "But the food is good and there's lots of it. Where are you from?"

"Canada. I'm going to Worcester, in the Midlands, where my grandparents live."

"We're going to the Midlands, too! Mom and me and my two younger brothers and baby sister are going to help our grandparents on their farm. My dad died this year and granddad is sick, so they need us."

"My dad died, too, but a long time ago."

Norman shakes his head. "It's tough," he says. "I'm in charge of my two brothers, Joseph and Abe. They're five and six and always into mischief. Abe jumped from the top bunk yesterday and almost cracked his head open. My baby sister is sweet though. Her name is Elizabeth but we call her Lizzie. She smiles all the time, except when she's hungry."

"My best friend's name is Lizzie and she smiles a lot, too."

Norman grins. He has dimples and a wide, toothy smile. "Have you ever been to England?" he asks.

"No. I hope I like it."

"I hope I do, too. Grandma says I'll be in charge of her chickens. I'll be gathering eggs every day and Grandma will teach me how to milk the cows. I've never taken care of chickens or cows. We're from New York City."

"Good luck," I say. "I'll think of you whenever I have scrambled eggs or drink milk. Who knows? They might come from your farm!"

Norman laughs. "They might."

"I'd better get back. Goodbye, Norman." I wave and head out of the dining room, down the hall and back up the stairs to second class.

Evening • Going, Going, Gone

WHEN I RETURN to the cabin, I tell Hilda and Sarah that I'm going to the show in first class with the professor. Hilda wants me to stay in the cabin and start packing. Sarah says I shouldn't be sneaking into first class. But I don't want to stay in the cabin with them. Not tonight. For the past few days they've avoided each other, but tonight they'll be together all evening and I don't want to hear their arguments or insults or — worse — feel their silence.

"It's almost my last night on the *Lusy* and I'm going," I tell them as I slip into the green dress that Hilda said looked good with my eyes. I want to look fancy for first class!

"The show's right after dinner. I won't be back late." Before they can protest, I'm out the door.

After dinner the professor and I hurry upstairs to first class. We pass crew members covering the lights, drawing the saloon curtains and darkening the port-holes and skylights.

"Now this *is* getting scary," I say to the professor.

"Let's not worry. It's a wise move and a good precaution," he says.

I know the professor is trying to keep me calm. I know he's trying to feel calm himself, but no matter how hard we try, we can't escape the mood on the ship. People are anxious about tomorrow. No one knows what will happen. Everyone will be relieved when we reach shore early Saturday morning.

We slip into the first-class saloon. No one notices us or cares that we don't belong. A Welsh choir is singing. Then a band plays. After that a man plays a piano and sings "I Love a Piano" by Irving Berlin. Some passengers recite poems and do magic tricks. Others tell jokes, but most of them are awful.

"Your jokes were much better," I whisper to the professor.

The captain stands up to speak, and an uneasy hush descends on the room. "There has been a warning of submarine action in the area we're approaching," he says.

People gasp. He's telling us what we all feared most.

"But there's no need for alarm," he quickly continues. "When we enter the war zone tomorrow, the British navy will be there, waiting for us. They will make sure we arrive safely. So it's full steam ahead for

Liverpool. We will make it on time — early the next morning. Gentlemen, please extinguish your cigarettes on deck tonight. Just a precaution. Goodnight and see you in the morning."

The captain leaves but the mood is still grim. People cluster in small groups. One man insists he will sleep on deck till we reach shore. He plans to be dressed and ready for anything. Some people decide to sleep in the public rooms for the rest of the trip. The stewards hustle to find them blankets and pillows.

It's late. So we leave.

"Wish me luck with the Hilda and Sarah war," I tell the professor. "There may be screaming. There may be insults. There may be bottles and hair brushes thrown. And if not it will be very, very quiet in our cabin."

"You can handle it," says the professor. "And remember, after tonight it's just one more night."

But when I return to the cabin, I'm shocked. Hilda and Sarah are sitting on Hilda's bed, chatting like old friends.

"It was all a silly misunderstanding," says Sarah. "I thought Hilda was laughing at my friendship with Peter and Hilda thought I was pleased that Richard was engaged. We are the best of friends again and we can't wait to have tea together in London. Perhaps you can join us, Avis."

"You want to have tea with me?" I ask.

"Absolutely," says Sarah. "We're all friends now, aren't we?"

I nod and smile at both of them. The war in our cabin is over!

I undress, slip into my nightgown, climb into my berth and pick up the small ship my father carved. I will put it in my pocket tomorrow morning where it will be safe. I close my eyes and pray that we will all be safe as we enter the war zone and head for shore.

Day Seven
Friday, May 7, 1915

Morning • I Can See It!

"I ALMOST FELL over the railing! You can't see anything out there!"

Sarah's voice wakes me up.

"A U-boat couldn't see anything in this thick fog," says Hilda. "I don't know why so many people are worried."

I open my eyes. Hilda and Sarah are dressed.

"How long have you been up?" I ask.

"For an hour. Neither of us could sleep so we walked out on deck," says Hilda.

"Didn't you hear the foghorn?" asks Sarah. "Imagine! It was so foggy that Peter and I didn't even recognize each other."

"Not till he stepped on your toes," says Hilda.

We all laugh. It feels good to laugh with them. I slide off my berth and dress. I put my little ship in my pocket and button it up. I'll show it to the professor after he tells me the end of the Foula story.

Hilda and Sarah sit on Hilda's berth and talk about London. They'll take the train from Liverpool to London as soon as they have seen me onto the train to my grandparents in Worcester.

"Your grandparents will be delighted to meet you for the first time," says Hilda. Her voice is soft and friendly.

"And you can come down and meet us in London when you have a holiday from school," says Sarah. She pats my hand. "We can take you to see the sights. Then we can have tea in an elegant cafe."

"I'd like that," I say. And to my surprise, it's true. If you asked me three days ago, I would have sworn that Hilda and Sarah were the last two people on earth I'd ever want to meet again. But something's changed. Is it me? Is it them? Is it being thrown together on the *Lusy* with so much happening to each of us? We've all met new people — the professor, Peter, Jane, Richard, Sam the bellboy, the Blooms, Norman McGuire. And soon we'll all go our separate ways.

"Come on, Avis. Let's have breakfast together," says Sarah. "We won't have much time for a leisurely breakfast before we dock tomorrow."

Arm in arm, we walk to the dining room. We all sit together — Sarah, Peter, Hilda, the Blooms and me. Peter still doesn't say much. Sarah still says too much, but the rest of us talk, eat and laugh.

When breakfast is over, Hilda and Sarah stroll on deck. Peter and the Blooms return to their cabins to pack, and so do I. The professor and I are meeting at eleven for a last morning walk. I can't wait to hear the end of the Foula story. I'm desperate to know what happens.

It doesn't take me long to pack. I'm finished at ten, and I dash out to the lounge to read my adventure story for an hour. As always, Sam is rushing around with a handful of messages. He bounds over.

"The fog's gone. We're out in the sea in full view now," he says. "I hope we make it to land."

"You never found Dowie, did you?" I ask.

"No. I'm sure he's back in New York, licking his whiskers after eating tasty mice on the dock."

"That's probably why he stayed. More mice to enjoy!"

"Maybe. But Dowie knew something was going to happen on this trip. I don't know what and I don't know when, but something will happen — I can feel it. I didn't sleep much last night. And now we're in the war zone. Can you feel the ship slowing down?"

"You're right. It does feel slower. I thought the captain said 'full steam ahead.' Why would we slow down?"

"I don't know. Lots of passengers have noticed, too, and they're worried. And I've looked and looked but I don't see any British ships around to escort us to shore. I couldn't eat breakfast today. My stomach feels like I've swallowed broken glass."

"We'll all feel better when we reach land."

Sam sighs. "You mean *if* we reach land."

I walk outside to meet the professor. He's staring out to sea again.

"Good morning, Avis! Look! It's the coast of Ireland. You can't see it clearly yet but it's there. We're close now."

We peer out. The coast is faint in the distance. Just a smudge of green, but I can see a hill if I squint. Land is near!

"In less than twenty-four hours we'll be standing on shore," says the professor. "And we'll be saying goodbye to each other, but only for a little while. Marion and I will write to your grandparents as soon as we reach home. We'll arrange for you to visit us soon. You'll love my family and they'll love you. And of course you'll love Foula."

"I do already! So now tell me the end of Jill's story," I say.

"Oh dear, Avis. Can I tell you after lunch? I have to return to my cabin to organize a few things this morning. I'll tell you the end of the story right after dessert. I promise."

"Are you dragging the story out to build up the suspense again, Professor?" I ask, winking with my left eye.

"No, I'm not. I just want to make sure that I have all my notes and papers in order. Then I can take my time telling you the end of the Foula story. I promise. It's a good ending."

I roll my eyes. "If you forget I'll remind you."

The professor laughs and winks his right eye. "I know you will, Avis. I count on it."

Afternoon • Follow Me

I GO TO LUNCH at one, but the professor isn't there. Neither are Hilda or Sarah. Lunch is thick beef stew with tomatoes and onions. It's good, but I wish someone would show up to have dessert with me. It's the first time I've eaten alone. I've ordered something different today — pear and blanc mange. I'm not sure what blanc mange is.

"A delicious pudding with milk, cream and sugar," says the waiter. "You'll love it!"

Here comes the dessert, and it's a plate full of shiny creaminess. And there are Hilda and Sarah, arm in arm. Still friends. Hooray! That means it will be friendly in the cabin tonight. They wave as I lift my spoon to taste the blanc mange …

Oh my God! Oh my God!

The spoon flies out of my hand! The blanc mange topples to the floor. The table tilts. Chairs crash. What's happening? It can't be, but it feels like … like … an explosion?

Oh no! No! People are screaming, pushing their way out of the dining room. Where are Hilda and Sarah? Where's the professor? What should I do? He said to find him if …

Another explosion! Louder. Harder. I fall to the floor. We've been hit. I know it. What do I do now? Please come, Professor. Please.

"Avis, stay where you are. I'm coming."

I hear his voice or is it my imagination?

No. He's here beside me, helping me up.

"We've been torpedoed. There's no time to waste. The ship's sinking fast. Follow me."

We snake through the screaming crowds. The ship tilts so hard and so fast, we have to hold on to the rails to walk. We balance our feet against the wall to stay up. The halls jam with people. Crying. Begging. Looking for family and friends. Looking for lifeboats.

We plow our way through to the professor's cabin. He hands me a spare lifebelt. My hands shake as I strap myself into it. The professor checks it. Tightens it. Makes sure it's on right.

He wraps his important papers in an oilcloth and tucks them into his vest. He grabs his lifebelt, and we race out. The ship is tilting more and more. It feels like it will go under at any moment.

We climb over broken tables, chairs, lights, dishes, ripped jackets, skirts, underwear and tablecloths. We stumble over a pair of boots and a headless doll.

The injured are everywhere — sobbing, moaning — but we can't help them. We can't stop. I shudder as we step over a woman. I know her! She's Harold's wife, Mildred. Harold, who I met on the deck just two days ago. Harold, who can't swim. And here's his wife. Is she unconscious — or dead? We can't even stop to help her.

We hurry on and there are Hilda and Sarah, just steps away from us. They call out. We squeeze our way over to them. Hilda is wearing a lifebelt but Sarah is not.

"Take mine," says the professor. He thrusts his lifebelt into her hands.

Sarah shakes her head and hands it back. "No. You keep it. You have a family. I don't."

"You must take it," the professor insists.

"I can't wear the lifebelt. I couldn't breathe with it on. Water frightens me. Help us find a lifeboat," Sarah begs.

"Follow me!" says the professor.

We push on and see a lifeboat attached to the side of the ship. A stocky man with a black beard pulls out a revolver. He waves it at the crewmen.

"The ship is sinking, you fools. Launch this lifeboat or I'll shoot."

The terrified crewmen untie the lifeboat. It drops like a rock. It smashes against the side of the ship, shattering like glass, crushing people on the deck below. Their screams pierce through me like a knife, but there's no time to stop. No time to feel.

"Starboard!" the professor shouts over the screams.

Ahead of us, a young girl with long brown hair trips over a woman's body. She slides across the deck.

Oh no! She's going to be swept overboard, but just in time a steward grabs her, helps her up.

We keep going, going till we reach the starboard side of the ship — and a lifeboat! It's filling up. The professor quickly lifts me over the railing to help me across the gap. He kisses me on the cheek.

"Please kiss my wife and children for me," he says.

I want to shout, "No. Come with us. You have to come with us."

But I know he won't. He's going to jump.

I squeeze his hand. I try to tell him with my eyes what I feel. How good he has been to me. How much he matters.

He nods. He knows. He helps Hilda and Sarah into the lifeboat.

The lifeboat is lowered.

"Dear man," says Hilda. "We owe him so much."

Sarah nods but she's sobbing so hard, she's shaking. I grab her hand. Hilda grabs mine. We are going down, down.

I glance up to the deck. The professor is about to jump. My chest hurts like someone squeezed it, stepped on it.

"Oh no! No!" I cry.

Hilda puts her arm around me. Sarah sobs and sobs. He's gone.

Our boat sways. It drops lower. And lower. We're close to the sea. The *Lusy* looms over us. Its giant smokestacks tilt toward us.

And then two men leap into our boat from the deck of the *Lusy*.

OhmyGod. OhmyGod. OhmyGod.

The lifeboat cracks. We're tipping. Tipping. Tipping into the sea. I'm under. Icy water fills my nose. My ears. I hold my breath. The sea is dark. My feet and hands are numb. No. No. I can't die.

I kick. Kick. Hard. Harder. Fight. Yes! I'm up! Up! I spit out mouthfuls of salty ocean and seaweed. My stomach turns. My nose burns. The sun blinds me. I squint. My eyes sting. I can't feel my toes, my hands. Breathe. Breathe.

People cling to a chair leg, half a desk, a broken headboard, a sink. Some no longer cling. They float. Their eyes are lifeless.

OhmyGod! Is that the girl who smooched in the lifeboat floating beside me? I don't know. I can't see. The sun sears my eyes. I can't look, but I must look. For a boat. There must be a boat. Oh, Father! Professor! Jill! I won't give up. I won't.

My clothes and shoes drag me down. My head falls back. No! I can't let it. Stay up! Up!

Is that a boat? Yes! Yes! I call out. My voice squeaks, falters, fades. It's lost in the ocean. But the boat is close. Does the man in it see me? Please. See me!

Nothing. Is the boat there? Did I see it at all? Am I lost? Will I drift here till … till … No! No! I can't.

A jagged tabletop smashes against me. I grab it.

Cling to it. My hands are cold and slippery, but I hold on.

I call out again. "Help! I'm alive. This way. Please. Please! Hurry!"

Does anyone hear me? So many cry. So many scream. Birds squawk overhead. There is just so much noise.

OhmyGod! The *Lusy* is gone. Swallowed up by the sea. No. No. Don't think about that. Stay up. Hold on.

I tread water as fast as I can. I lift my head higher. Higher. I call out again and again. My voice is hoarse, but I don't stop. There is a boat. There has to be a boat. Oh no! The sun is too bright. I can't see anything.

Wait. There it is. I see it. Coming toward me. Yes! Yes! The man sees me. He waves his cap.

"Hold on," he shouts. "I'm coming."

"Yes. Yes. Here I am!" I call out. "Please. Hurry!"

Strong arms pull me out of the water. I collapse into a small inflatable boat. I can't stop shivering. The man in the boat wraps a blanket around my shoulders.

"You're fine," he says. "I'm James Kincaid. You're alive."

I am! I am!

"Thank you. Thank you," I repeat the words over and over.

I lean back in the tiny boat. I can't stop shaking. I take deep, long breaths. The air is cold, salty. It hurts to swallow.

Oh, Professor. I'm alive but where are you? I close my eyes. In my mind I see him jump again. I see him disappear under the waves.

He can't be dead. He's a strong swimmer. He loves the sea. He knows the sea. He'll fight to live. For his family. For me. To see Foula.

And Hilda and Sarah? Hilda has a lifebelt. Maybe she's been rescued, but poor Sarah. She hasn't a chance. She has no lifebelt. She's scared of water. She can't swim.

People drift past our boat, screaming, begging James to take them in.

Pain streaks his craggy, unshaven face. "I wish I could help them," he murmurs, "but I only have room for one."

I am the one.

A lump fills my throat. It's so big I can barely breathe. I'm safe, but what of all the people I knew on the *Lusy*? I scan the sea for Hilda, the professor, anyone I know, but I don't see anyone. It hurts to think of them. It aches to think of the professor. He can't be gone. I feel like I've lost my father all over again.

I remember the small ship Father carved for me. My hand trembles as I touch my pocket. Yes, there's a lump there. It must be the ship, but did it break? I unfasten my pocket and slowly pull it out. I can't believe it. This tiny ship survived. It's wet, but it's in one piece! I wipe it off with a dry corner of the blanket. I hold Father's ship. I stroke it.

I look out again. The body of a young girl floats past me. I feel sick to my stomach. I bite my lip but tears explode from my eyes. I sob.

"There, there," says James, patting my shoulder. "Don't look. It doesn't help. It breaks my heart that I can't save anyone else. But my boat is so small. There are other, bigger boats out there. Maybe more people will be rescued alive. I hope so."

I wipe my eyes. "Thank you," I mutter. "It's not your fault you have no room. You came to help. Thank you."

James nods and wipes a tear from his eye. "Now rest. We will be on land soon. You'll want to get out of those wet clothes and have a hot cup of tea."

James is right. I have to get out of my dirty, damp clothes. I touch my hair. It's matted down with oil and grease and seaweed and who knows what else. I shudder.

I close my eyes. It hurts too much to look at the sea anymore. It hurts too much to remember all those people I met on the *Lusy* who may be dead, lying at the bottom of the ocean — Mr. and Mrs. Bloom, Sam the bellboy, Harold, Peter, Norman McGuire, his mom, brothers and little sister, Lizzie. The *Lusy* sank so fast. It took only minutes. And so few lifeboats worked. Just like the professor predicted.

Is Captain Turner alive, or did he go down with the ship, like Captain Smith of the *Titanic*? If Captain Turner is alive, does he remember the professor's warning? Is he regretting his actions? Is he heartbroken about that giant, magnificent ship lying in pieces at the bottom of the sea with so many innocent people inside her?

"Here we are," says James.

I open my eyes. We're near a dock. Somewhere near Queenstown, says James. He extends his hand and helps me climb ashore. My legs are weak. Shaky. I wobble. I trip. I almost fall. James grabs me by the waist. He helps me stand up.

"No young person should have to live through this. No young person should see all that death and know how evil the world can be," he says.

"But there's goodness, too," I say. "You came to help."

"Many others came, too. We had to do something. Each life is important."

I bite my lip again, trying to stop tears from gushing out of my eyes. I know my tears make James sad. I can see it in his eyes. He's been so good. His kindness reminds me of the professor. I owe them both so much.

"My name is Avis. Avis Dolphin," I tell him.

James's lips curl into a smile. "A pleasure to meet you, Avis Dolphin."

We walk into a small fishing hut. There's a stove, some rickety wooden chairs and a few people. It smells of fish, wood, smoke and sweat. Two fishermen and a family of three they've just rescued sip tea to warm up.

"Here's a rug to wrap around you. You'll want to take off those wet clothes and let them dry by the stove," says James.

I wrap the large gray and red rug around me and slip off my dress, my underwear, my shoes. The rug feels rough and scratchy against my skin, but I don't care. I'm dry — not soaked through to my bones. I can't do much about my hair though. Not in the hut. There's no water to wash the grease, the oil and the grime off. My hair is disgusting, and for an instant I remember Hilda's perfect hair and how she'd give me her look if she saw mine today. But maybe she wouldn't. Maybe she'd understand that sometimes it doesn't matter. What matters is being alive. Oh, Hilda. Are you alive?

I drape my clothing on a chair near the hot stove. I balance on a wobbly wooden chair beside it. James hands me a cup of strong tea with milk and sugar. My tongue and throat burn from swallowing seawater. I sip the tea slowly. It hurts my throat but it warms me, like the scratchy rug around me. I move closer to the stove. I wiggle my fingers and toes. I can feel them for the first time since I was plunged into the ocean.

I glance at the family in the corner. A young boy with big green eyes and long black eyelashes snuggles against his mother. She strokes his hair. She gazes at him with such tenderness, my eyes well up with tears again.

"Your brother is gone, William," she murmurs,

"but God spared you and we're grateful. So grateful."
William's father holds his hand and stares at him as
if he can't believe he's alive.

I wipe my tears away with my tea-warmed hands,
but my tears won't stop. They dribble down my
cheeks. I turn to James, sitting on a wooden chair
beside me and drinking tea. I wipe my eyes again.

"I have to find someone," I stammer. "Someone
special to me. I have to know if he's alive. Can you
help me? Please. His name is Professor Ian Holbourn. And if you hear anything about Hilda Ellis
and Sarah Smith, I have to know what happened to
them, too."

"I'll ask around the city after I finish my tea. I
promise, Avis. But so many didn't make it," he says.
"You need to be prepared for the worst."

I shake my head. "I understand, but I have to know
about the professor."

"If I can find an answer for you, I will."

James puts on his fisherman's cap and tips it toward me. My heart almost stops. It's like the professor tipping his cap the day he met me on the dock
and saved me from being trampled by that horse.

Oh, Professor. Please be alive. Please!

Evening • The Ending

IF FEELS LIKE hours have gone by since James left.
I'm warm now, and all the numbness has left my fin-

gers and toes. My clothes are almost dry. They reek of the sea and damp, but I wear them anyway and sit by the fire to dry them off more.

I can't stop thinking about what happened just a few hours ago. I can't stop picturing how the sea swept me under. How I fought to stay up and tried and prayed to be rescued. I can't stop seeing all those bodies, all those injured, all the bits and pieces of the ship floating around me. I can't stop hearing the voices.

The family of three stand up. "Goodbye, young lady. Good luck," says little William's mother. "Do you have somewhere to go?"

"Yes. Thank you and good luck to you, too," I say as they leave.

One fisherman remains in the hut and promises he won't leave me till James returns. His name is Alfred.

When will James come back? What if the professor is dead? What if Hilda and Sarah are dead? How will I bear it? How will I travel to my grandparents? I have to let them know I'm alive. And Mother in Canada. Thoughts race around and around in my head. I tell myself I'll figure it out. People will help me find my way. But my head keeps whirling, whirling.

Alfred makes soup and offers me a bowl. My stomach aches but my throat stings less now, and I sip the hot soup full of potatoes and onions. It warms me.

I picture all those meals on the *Lusy*. The stews and soups and scrambled eggs and pancakes and puddings and ice cream. I picture the elevator ride up to first class and what fun the professor and I had sneaking into the dining room and gawking at the rich enjoying their sumptuous platters of food. I smile remembering how we were almost kicked out of first class by the angry waiter. Where is that waiter now? Where are all those waiters and cooks?

And the first-class elevator man? And the German stowaways, especially the young one who looked at me with such sad eyes? The professor was sure they'd never make it out alive if the ship sank. And what about the crewmen near the lifeboats? And the couples who hid in the lifeboats kissing and hugging? And Ailsa who won the spelling contest and was so proud? And the people playing shuffleboard? And Norman from third class who was going to work on his grandparents' farm? And his family?

And what about Mr. Vanderbilt who came to the professor's talk and stood up and cheered? The newspapermen on the dock said, "The rich die like the rest of us." Did Mr. Vanderbilt die or did he leap into a lifeboat? Is he at a hotel eating a delicious meal and wearing a pink carnation in his buttonhole?

If only I could shut out my thoughts. It hurts to remember all those people. Some of them had to make it out alive. But I know that most probably didn't. They couldn't. The ship sank too fast.

Stop thinking! There's nothing you can do. Think of Foula. Beautiful, far-away, rocky Foula. I close my eyes and picture Jill standing on the cliff, trapped between the giant and the bogeyman. I start to finish the story in my head. I'm so deep into the ending that I almost forget it's not the real ending. It's just my ending.

Oh, Professor, you have to tell me what really happens next. You promised you would and then … the world turned upside down. Oh, Professor, please, please be alive.

"Avis?"

I look up. It's James.

"Did you hear? Do you know?" I ask.

James's face breaks into a big smile. "Your friend Professor Holbourn is alive, Avis. He's weak and injured, but alive. He was stranded in the ocean with just his lifebelt for hours, clinging to a broken piece of a lifeboat, but he was finally picked up. I'm going to take you to see him now. He put the word out about you, too. He's desperate to see you."

"Oh, James. Thank you! Again!"

I throw my arms around him. James blushes and laughs. I dance around the fishing hut. James and his friend clap their hands and guffaw. James pats me on the back and blushes even more.

I thank Alfred, and James and I hurry out. I follow him down the dark streets. We walk and walk. My feet throb like I've climbed a mountain, but I don't care. The professor is alive and I'm going to see him!

"Here's the hotel where they've brought him," says James. We hurry inside and are directed up to the second floor. Room 8. We knock.

"Come in," says a voice. I want to shout for joy. I know that voice. I know that Scottish accent.

I open the door and run to the professor. He's sitting up in bed. He's pale. His face is cut and bruised. There's a big lump on his forehead, but he's smiling. I throw my arms around him and burst into tears. I can't help it. The professor pats my back. He cries, too. He wipes his tears, but they dribble down his face. We cry. We laugh. We joke. We hug.

James says he will secure me a room in the hotel. Then he will be off.

"Thank you for saving my dear friend Avis," says the professor. "We owe you our eternal gratitude. My wife is coming to collect us both and we will take Avis to her grandparents."

I run over and hug James again. He blushes again and says, "It was an honor to help you." Then he turns to go.

"Wait! I forgot to ask you. Have you heard anything about Hilda Ellis or Sarah Smith?"

James shakes his head. "They're not listed among the survivors but that doesn't mean they won't be found. There's always a chance. But I won't lie to you. There's not a big chance. The boats out now are only returning with bodies. I'm sorry."

"What of Mr. Vanderbilt?" asks the professor.

"They say he died on the ship but his body hasn't been found yet. He was a gentleman and a hero. He and his valet saved people's lives. They marshaled them into lifeboats, cool as cucumbers. Never thought of their own safety," says James. "Sometimes the rich surprise you."

"He and his valet were gentlemen in the best sense of the word," says the professor. He takes a deep breath and swallows hard.

For a minute I can't talk. The lump in my throat is back and it stings like I've just swallowed a pitcher of sea water. Hilda and Sarah are probably dead. I know I'll hear more sad news in the next few days about people I knew on the *Lusy*.

Was it only seven days ago that I stood on that dock, scared and excited about the trip? Was it only seven days ago that I heard the warning about torpedoes ready to attack a passenger ship? It seems like it was months ago, years ago.

"There's nothing more we can do," says James, "except remember the people who are lost. All those innocent people who died on that ship." James tips his cap. "I wish you a long, happy life, Avis Dolphin," he says. "And you too, Professor." Then he's gone.

For a few minutes the professor and I say nothing. Finally, I turn to him. "Well, it's time," I say.

"Time, Avis? For what?"

"It's time for you to tell me the end of the Foula

story. I said I'd remind you and I am. Remember. You promised. I have to know what happens to Jill."

"I did promise. Unfortunately a torpedo got in the way of that promise and now I'm so tired, Avis. Too tired today to tell a story the way it deserves to be told. Why don't you tell me the ending instead?"

"Me? I don't know what happens. I've never been on Foula."

"Yes. You have. I've watched you as I've told you Jill's story. You've been there with me through every twist in the tale. You walked on Foula with Jill. You met the giant and the bogeyman. You know Jill as well as I do. It's your story now, too."

I take a deep breath. "I do have an ending. I thought of one while I waited to hear news about people on the *Lusy*. Most of all news about you, Professor. It's probably not the right ending. It just came to me."

"It's as right as any ending, Avis. That's the way stories are. They come to us when we need them most. So tell me, Avis. What happens next?"

"OK, Professor. Here goes." I wink with my left eye. "You know it will probably be a happy ending."

The professor winks back with his right eye. "That sounds perfect to me."

So I begin.

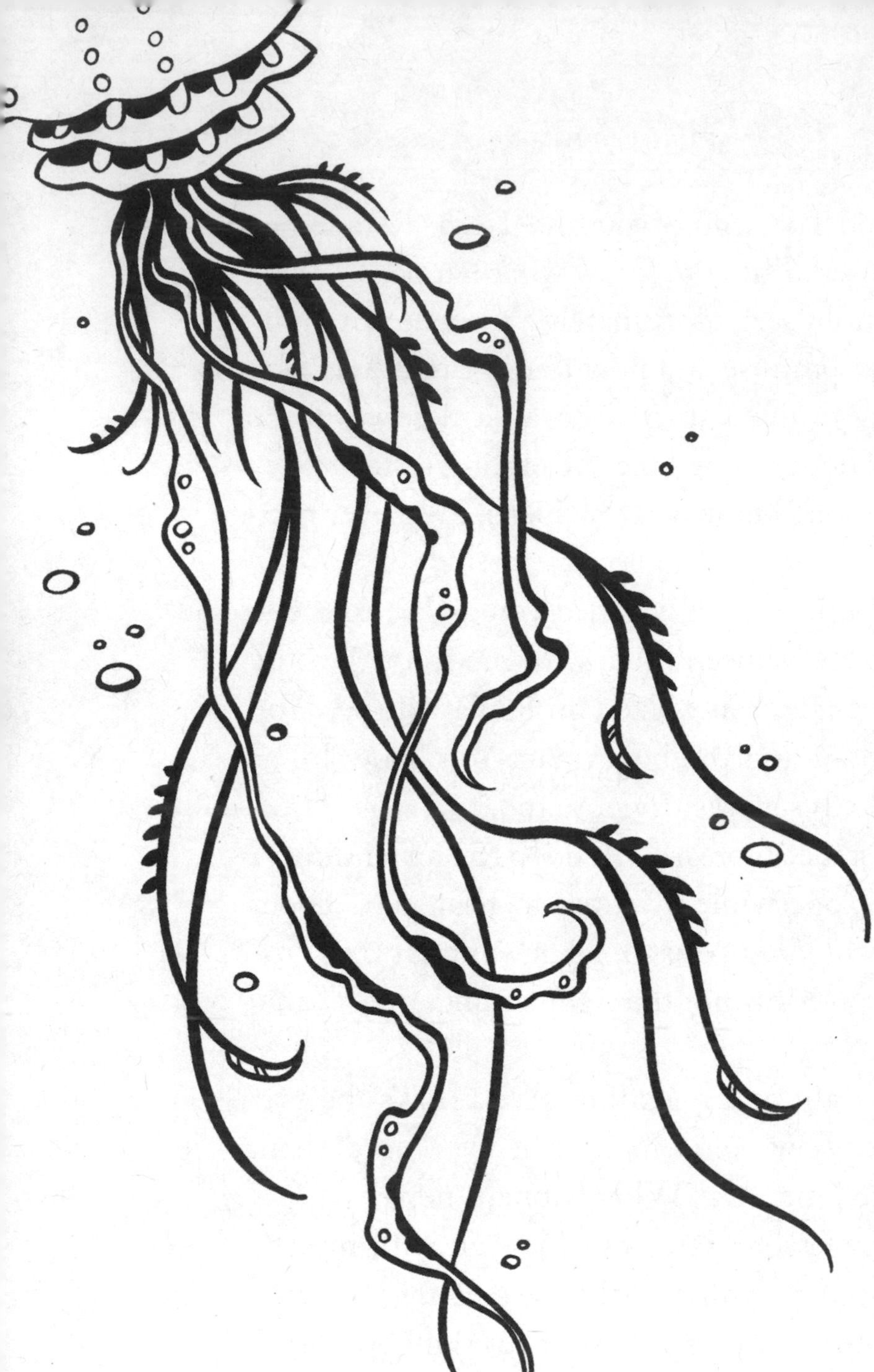

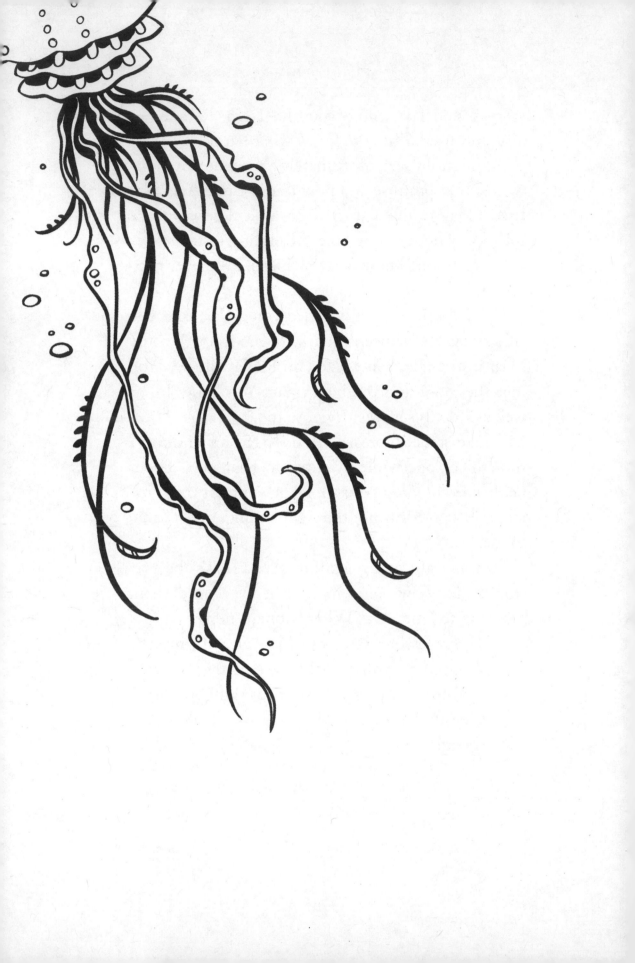

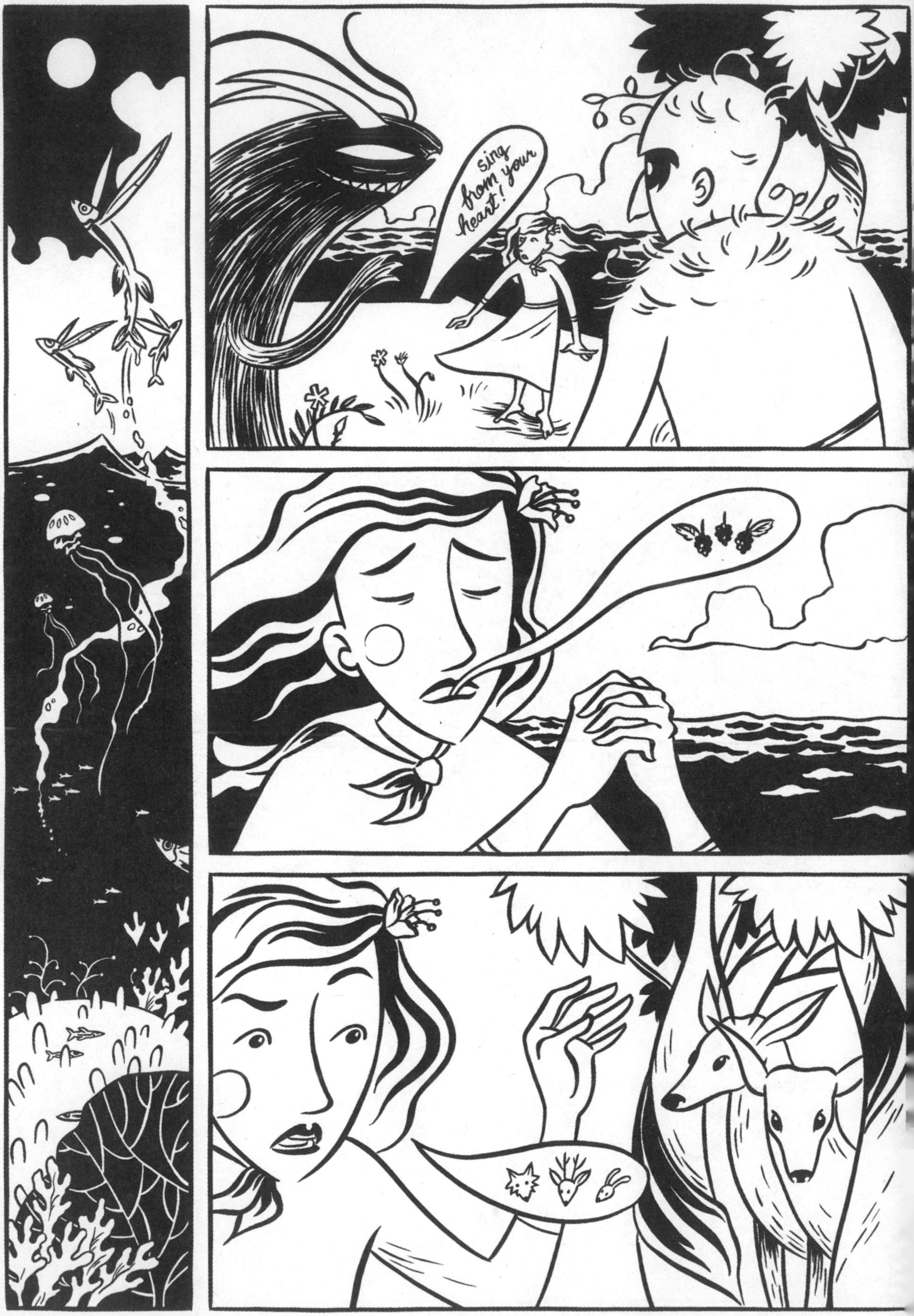
sing from your heart!

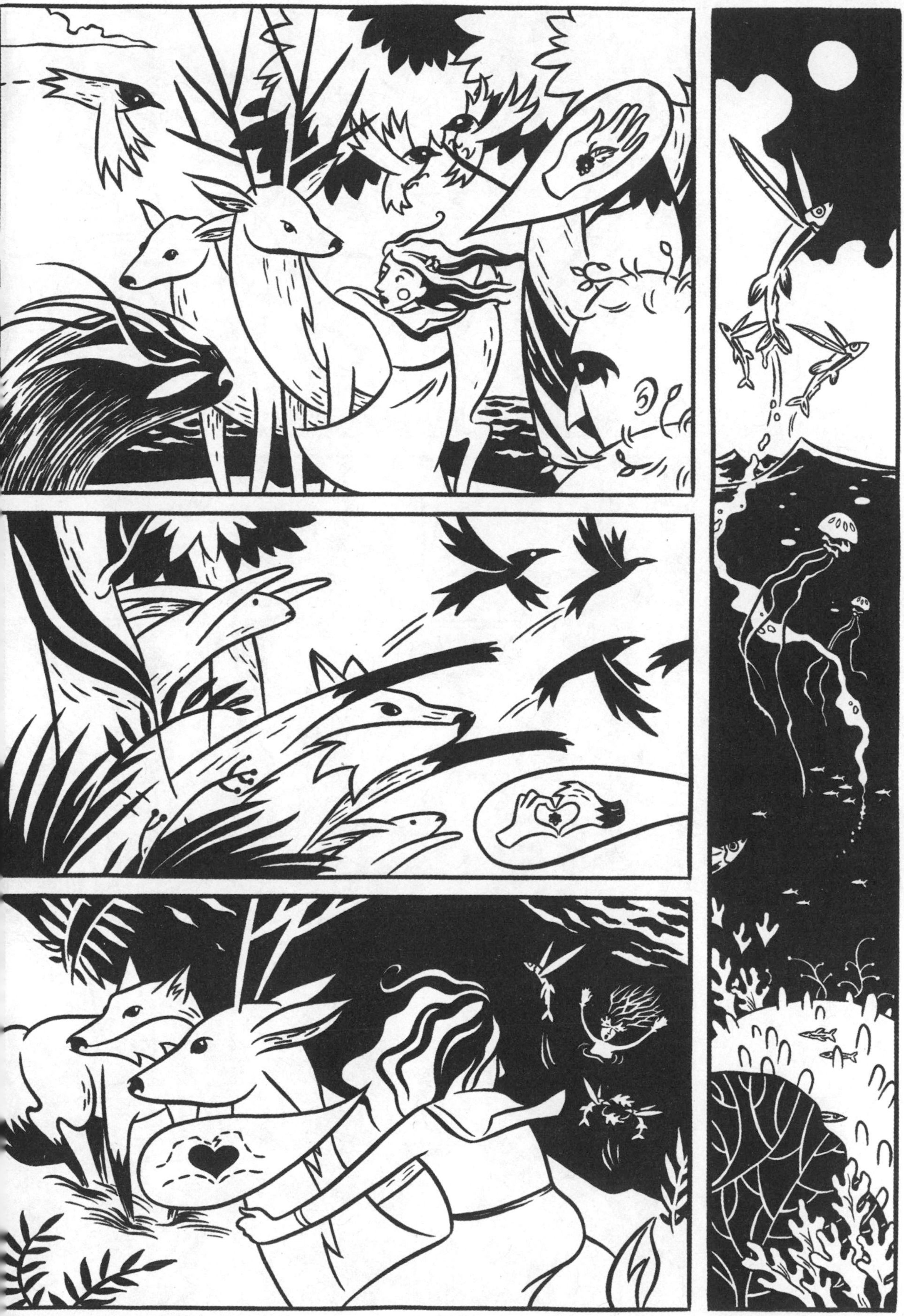

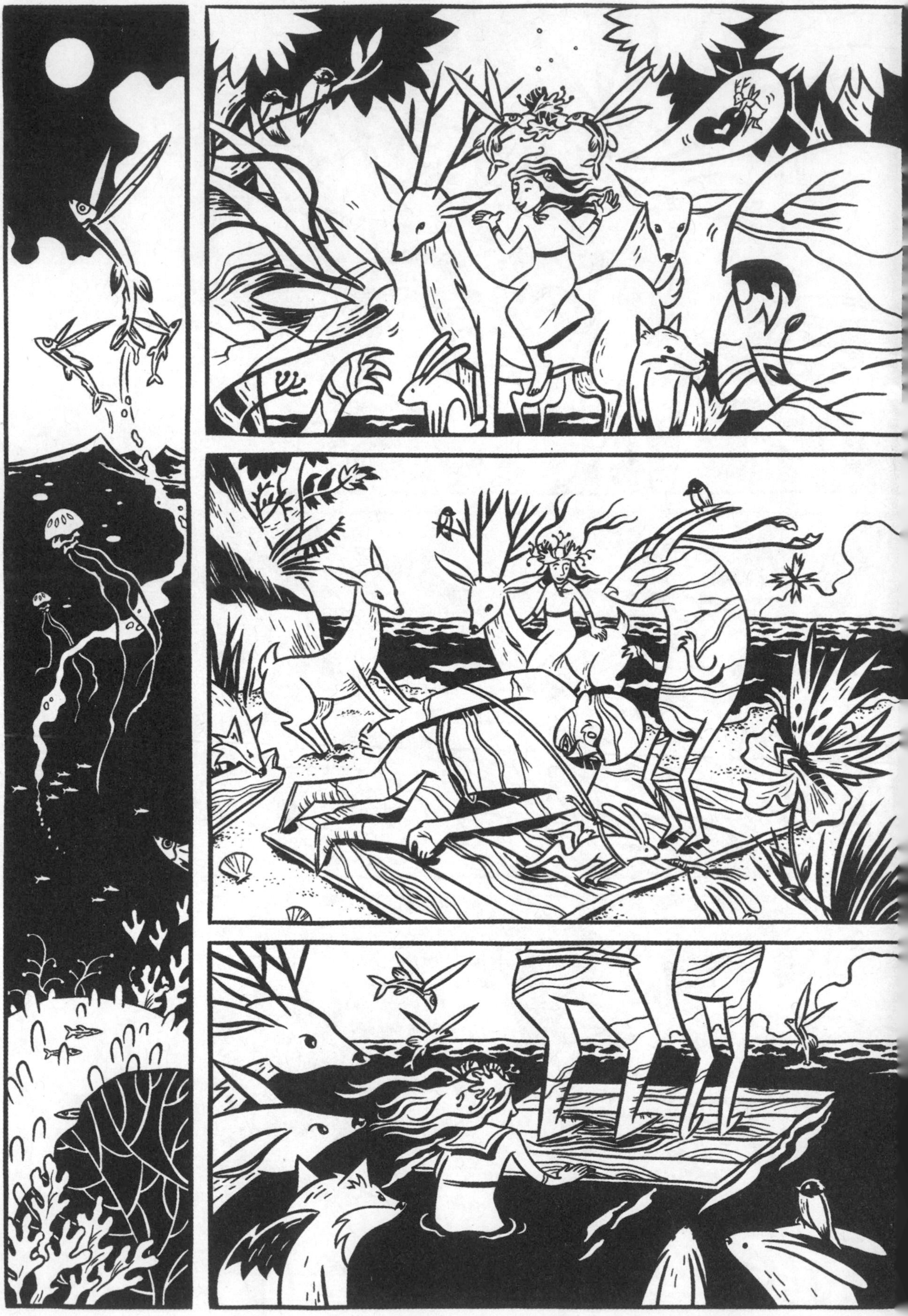

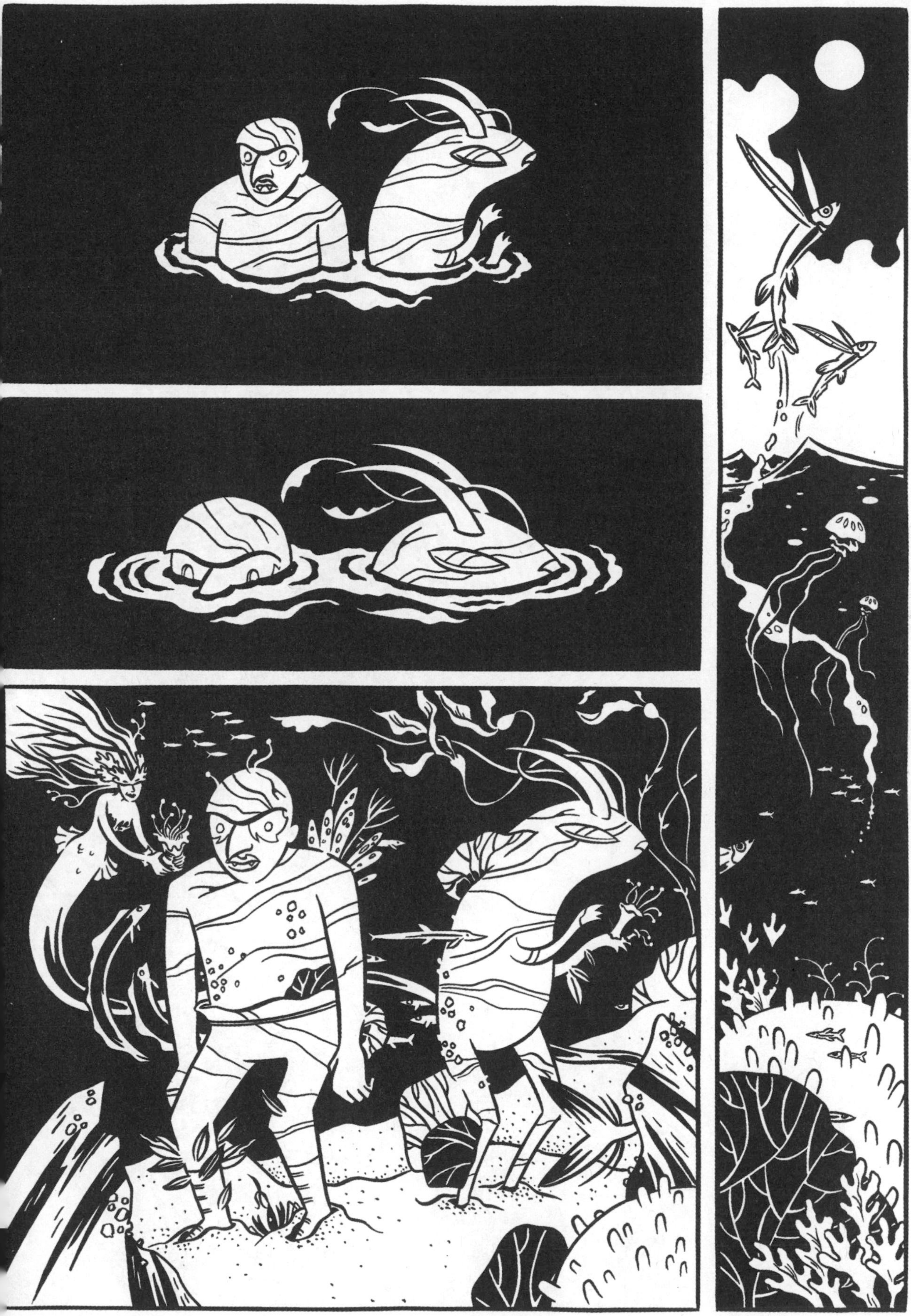

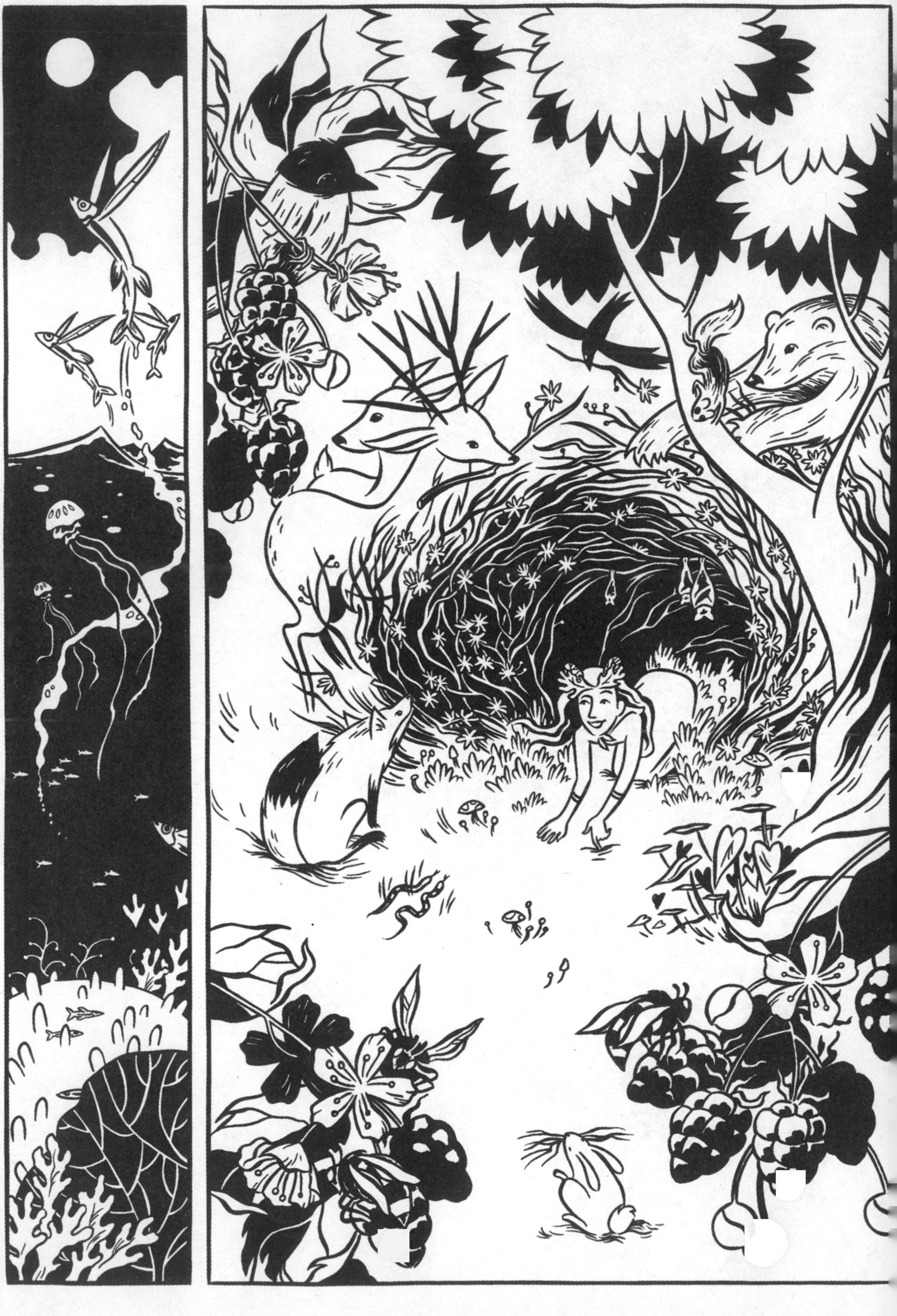

Afterword

THEY NEVER FOUND Hilda or Sarah. They never found Mr. Vanderbilt. They never found any of the other people I knew on the *Lusy*. The captain survived, and there was an inquiry about what happened to the *Lusitania* and who, besides the Germans, was responsible. Some people blamed the captain for making mistakes, but some people didn't.

More than 1,955 people sailed on the *Lusy*. Only about 760 survived. I know it's a miracle that the professor and I are alive. I feel it every day. And I know that if I hadn't met the professor, my life would have been different. He's family now. So are Marion and his boys.

As for Foula, it's not exactly the way I imagined it.

It's even more beautiful, more wonderful, more magical than that.

Author's Note

About World War I (1914–1918)

On June 28, 1914, Archduke Franz Ferdinand of Austria-Hungary and his wife, Sophie, were assassinated by a Serbian activist. That event and simmering disputes over land and power in Europe ignited World War I a month later.

Soon the Allied powers of France, Russia, Britain and its dominions of Australia, Canada, New Zealand and South Africa were fighting the Central powers of Germany, Austria-Hungary and, eventually, the Ottoman Empire. The United States joined the war in 1917.

Many people thought the war would end quickly. Young men marched off hoping for glory and easy victories. But by mid 1915 a different reality set in: Germany used chlorine gas as a chemical weapon, horrific battles were fought in which thousands were injured or killed by bullets, and thousands more soldiers died from disease in dirty, rat-infested trenches.

In February 1915, Germany declared the waters around the British Isles a war zone and threatened ships in the area. On May 1, 1915, Germany sank an American merchant ship, the *Gulflight*, off the British coast.

On May 7, 1915, the *Lusitania* was torpedoed by a German submarine and sank in eighteen minutes.

After many more bloody battles and millions of civilian and military casualties on both sides, World War I finally ended on November 11, 1918, with the defeat of the German army.

Who was the inspiration for Avis Dolphin?

While this book is fiction, and the characters are all drawn from my imagination, I was inspired by the experiences of the real Avis Dolphin, a twelve-year-old girl who sailed on the *Lusitania* in May 1915 and was befriended by Professor Ian Holbourn. Other characters in the novel — Hilda Ellis, Sarah Smith, Captain Turner and Alfred Vanderbilt — are also based on real people who took that fateful voyage, but many characters, such as Sam the bellboy, Peter, Mr. and Mrs. Bloom and Norman McGuire, are completely fictional.

WHAT HAPPENED TO THE REAL AVIS AND THE REAL PROFESSOR HOLBOURN?

After the sinking of the *Lusitania* Professor Holbourn and his wife, Marion, escorted Avis to her grandparents in Worcester. But Avis and the professor remained friends for life.

When Avis once complained that there were no good adventure stories for girls, Professor Holbourn wrote *The Child of the Moat* and dedicated it to her. The book sold well but before it could be reprinted the publisher went bankrupt.

Professor Holbourn continued to teach, write, and travel to the United States. He was shipwrecked again in 1929 when he was caught in a storm. He was injured but survived that disaster, too. Ian Holbourn died on September 14, 1935.

After Avis finished school, she moved to Edinburgh to be closer to the Holbourns. She met her future husband, Thomas Foley, while visiting them. She lived in Wales for the rest of her life and died on February 5, 1996.

AND WHAT ABOUT FOULA?

Foula is one of the most remote, inhabited islands in the western Scottish Shetlands. It has five spectacular peaks, as well as rocks, peat banks, coarse grass and a tiny beach. It is populated by a small number of people and lots of birds. The name Foula means "bird island," and passionate birdwatchers flock there to view the many thousands of birds from a variety of species.

Professor Ian Holbourn was the last Laird of Foula, but members of his family continue to live on the island. One of his descendants, Penny Gear, explained why she returned to Foula after living on the mainland for seventeen years: "I love the freedom, the beauty, the nature, the life. Sometimes I walk over to the headland just to see the rollers coming in. It's breathtaking, always."

FRIEDA WISHINSKY is the award-winning author of more than sixty books, including picture books, novels and non-fiction. Her books have been translated into many languages, and *Please, Louise!* won the Marilyn Baillie Picture Book Award. Frieda's recent books are *Explorers Who Made It … or died trying* and *A History of Just About Everything*, written with Elizabeth MacLeod. Frieda loves sharing the writing process with students at all levels. She lives in Toronto.

Award-winning author and illustrator WILLOW DAWSON's books include *Ghost Limb*, *Hyena in Petticoats*, *The Big Green Book of the Big Blue Sea* with Helaine Becker, *Lila and Ecco's Do-It-Yourself Comics Club*, *No Girls Allowed* with Susan Hughes, and *The Wolf-Birds* (forthcoming). Willow also teaches Creating Comics and Graphic Novels at the University of Toronto's School of Continuing Studies. She lives in Toronto.